HANS ANDERSEN'S
FAIRY TALES

CAXTON JUNIOR CLASSICS

HANS ANDERSEN'S FAIRY TALES

BY HANS CHRISTIAN ANDERSEN

ILLUSTRATED BY CHARLES MOZLEY

THE CAXTON PUBLISHING COMPANY LIMITED

LONDON · NEW YORK · MELBOURNE

TORONTO · WELLINGTON

This book was designed and produced by
George Rainbird Limited
2 Hyde Park Place, London W. 2
and was printed in Hungary by
Kossuth Printing House

Contents

The Mermaid

Far out at sea the water is as blue as the bluest cornflower, and as clear as the clearest crystal; but it is very deep, too deep for any cable to fathom, and if many steeples were piled on the top of one another they would not reach from the bed of the sea to the surface of the water. It is down there that the Mermen live.

Now don't imagine that there are only bare white sands at the bottom; oh no! the most wonderful trees and plants grow there, with such flexible stalks and leaves, that at the slightest motion of the water they move just as if they were alive. All the fish, big and little, glide among the branches just as, up here, birds glide through the air. The palace of the Merman King lies in the very deepest part; its walls are of coral and the long pointed windows of the clearest amber, but the roof is made of mussel shells which open and shut with the lapping of the water. This has a lovely effect, for there are gleaming pearls in every shell, any one of which would be the pride of a queen's crown.

The Merman King had been for many years a widower, but his old mother kept house for him; she was a clever woman, but so proud of her noble birth that she wore twelve oysters on her tail, while the other grandees were only allowed six. Otherwise she was worthy of all praise, especially because she was so fond of the little mermaid princesses, her grandchildren. They were six beautiful children, but the youngest was the prettiest of all, her skin was as soft and delicate as a rose leaf, her eyes as blue as the deepest sea, but like all the others she had no feet, and instead of legs she had a fish's tail.

All the livelong day they used to play in the palace in the great halls, where living flowers grew out of the walls. When the great amber windows were thrown open the fish swam in, just as the swallows fly into our rooms when we open the windows, but the fish swam right up to the little princesses, ate out of their hands, and allowed themselves to be patted.

Outside the palace was a large garden, with fiery red and deep blue trees, the fruit of which shone like gold, while the flowers glowed like fire on their ceaselessly waving stalks. The ground was of the finest sand, but it was of a blue phosphorescent tint. Everything was bathed in a wondrous blue light down there; you might more readily have supposed yourself to be high up in the air, with only the sky above and below you, than that you were at the bottom of the ocean. In a dead calm you could just catch a glimpse of the sun like a purple flower with a stream of light radiating from its calyx.

Each little princess had her own little plot of garden, where she could dig and plant just as she liked. One made her flower bed in the shape of a whale, another thought it nice to have hers like a little mermaid; but the youngest made hers quite round like the sun, and she would only have flowers of a rosy hue like its beams. She was a curious child, quiet and thoughtful, and while the other sisters decked out their gardens with all kinds of extraordinary objects which they got from wrecks, she would have nothing besides the rosy flowers like the sun up above, except a statue of a beautiful boy. It was hewn out of the purest white marble and had gone to the bottom from some wreck. By the statue she planted a rosy red

weeping willow which grew splendidly, and the fresh delicate branches hung round and over it, till they almost touched the blue sand where the shadows showed violet, and were ever moving like the branches. It looked as if the leaves and the roots were playfully interchanging kisses.

Nothing gave her greater pleasure than to hear about the world of human beings up above; she made her old grandmother tell her all that she knew about ships and towns, people and animals. But above all it seemed strangely beautiful to her that up on the earth the flowers were scented, for they were not so at the bottom of the sea; also that the woods were green, and that the fish which were to be seen among the branches could sing so loudly and sweetly that it was a delight to listen to them. You see the grandmother called little birds fish, or the mermaids would not have understood her, as they had never seen a bird.

"When you are fifteen," said the grandmother, "you will be allowed to rise up from the sea and sit on the rocks in the moonlight, and look at the big ships sailing by, and you will also see woods and towns."

One of the sisters would be fifteen in the following year, but the others—well, they were each one year younger than the other, so that the youngest had five whole years to wait before she would be allowed to come up from the bottom, to see what things were like on earth. But each one promised the others to give a full account of all that she had seen, and found most wonderful on the first day. Their grandmother could never tell them enough, for there were so many things about which they wanted information.

None of them was so full of longings as the youngest, the very one who had the longest time to wait, and who was so quiet and dreamy. Many a night she stood by the open windows and looked up through the dark blue water which the fish were lashing with their tails and fins. She could see the moon and the stars, it is true, their light was pale, but they looked much bigger through the water than they do to our eyes. When she saw a dark shadow glide between her and them, she knew that it was either a whale swimming above her, or else a ship laden with human beings. I am certain they never dreamt that a lovely little mermaid was standing down below, stretching up her white hands towards the keel.

The eldest princess had now reached her fifteenth birthday, and was to venture above the water. When she came back she had hundreds of things to tell them, but the most delightful of all, she said, was to lie in the moonlight, on a sandbank in a calm sea, and to gaze at the large town close to the shore, where the lights twinkled like hundreds of stars; to listen to music and the noise and bustle of carriages and people, to see the many church towers and spires, and to hear the bells ringing; and just because she could not go on shore she longed for that most of all.

Oh! how eagerly the youngest sister listened, and when, later in the evening she stood at the open window and looked up through the dark blue water, she thought of the big town with all its noise and bustle, and fancied that she could even hear the church bells ringing.

The year after, the second sister was allowed to mount up through the water and swim about wherever she liked. The sun was just going down when she reached the surface, the most beautiful sight, she thought, that she had ever seen. The whole sky had looked like gold, she said, and as for the clouds! well, their beauty was beyond description, they floated in red and violet splendour over her head, and, far faster than they went, a flock of wild swans flew like a long white veil over the water towards the setting sun; she swam towards it, but it sank and all the rosy light on clouds and water faded away.

The year after that the third sister went up, and being much the most venturesome of them all, swam up a broad river which ran into the sea. She saw beautiful green, vine-clad hills; palaces and country seats peeping through splendid woods. She heard the birds singing, and the sun was so hot that she was often obliged to dive, to cool her burning face. In a tiny bay she found a troop of little children running about naked and paddling in the water; she wanted to play with them, but they were frightened and ran away. Then a little black animal came up, it was a dog, but she had never seen one before; it barked so furiously at her that she was frightened and made for the open sea. She could never forget the beautiful woods, the green hills and the lovely children who could swim in the water although they had no fishes' tails.

The fourth sister was not so brave, she stayed in the remotest part of the ocean, and, according to her account, that was the most beautiful spot. You could see for miles and miles around you, and the sky above was like a great glass dome. She had seen ships, but only far away, so that they looked like sea-gulls. There were grotesque dolphins turning somersaults, and gigantic whales squirting water through their nostrils like hundreds of fountains on every side.

Now the fifth sister's turn came. Her birthday fell in the winter, so that she saw sights that the others had not seen on their first trips. The sea looked quite green, and large icebergs were floating about, each one of which looked like a pearl, she said, but was much bigger than the church towers built by men. They took the most wonderful shapes, and sparkled like diamonds. She had seated herself on one of the largest, and all the passing ships sheered off in alarm when they saw her sitting there with her long hair streaming in the wind.

In the evening the sky became overcast with dark clouds; it thundered and lightened, and the huge icebergs glittering in the bright lightning, were lifted high into the air by the black waves. All the ships shortened sail, and there was fear and trembling on every side, but she sat quietly on her floating iceberg watching the blue lightning flash in zigzags down on to the shining sea.

The first time any of the sisters rose above the water she was delighted by the novelties and beauties she saw; but once grown up, and at liberty to go where she liked, she became indifferent and longed for her home; in the course of a month or so they all said that after all their own home in the deep was best, it was so cosy there.

Many an evening the five sisters interlacing their arms would rise above the water together. They had lovely voices, much clearer than any mortal, and when a storm was rising, and they expected ships to be wrecked, they would sing in the most seductive strains of the wonders of the deep, bidding the seafarers have no fear of them. But the sailors could not understand the words, they thought it was the voice of the storm; nor could it be theirs to see this Elysium of the deep, for when the ship sank they were drowned, and only reached the Merman's palace in death. When the elder sisters rose up in this manner, arm-in-arm, in the evening, the youngest remained behind quite alone, looking after them as if she must weep, but mermaids have no tears and so they suffer all the more.

"Oh! if I were only fifteen!" she said, "I know how fond I shall be of the world above, and of the mortals who dwell there."

At last her fifteenth birthday came.

"Now we shall have you off our hands," said her grandmother, the old queen dowager. "Come now, let me adorn you like your other sisters!" and she put a wreath of white lilies round her hair, but every petal of the flowers was half a pearl; then the old queen had eight oysters fixed on to the princess's tail to show her high rank.

"But it hurts so!" said the little mermaid.

"You must endure the pain for the sake of the finery!" said her grandmother.

But oh! how gladly would she have shaken off all this splendour, and laid aside the heavy wreath. Her red flowers in her garden suited her much better, but she did not dare to make any alteration. "Good-bye," she said, and mounted as lightly and airily as a bubble through the water.

The sun had just set when her head rose above the water, but the clouds were still lighted up with a rosy and golden splendour, and the evening star sparkled in the soft pink sky, the air was mild and fresh, and the sea as calm as a millpond. A big three-masted ship lay close by with only a single sail set, for there was not a breath of wind, and the sailors were sitting about the rigging, on the cross-trees, and at the mastheads. There was music and singing on board, and as the evening closed in, hundreds of gaily coloured lanterns were lighted —they looked like the flags of all nations waving in the air. The little mermaid swam right up to the cabin windows, and every time she was lifted by the swell she could see through the transparent panes crowds of gaily dressed people. The handsomest of them all was the young prince with large dark eyes; he could not be much more than sixteen, and all these festivities were in honour of his birthday. The sailors danced on deck, and when the prince appeared among them hundreds of rockets were let off making it as light as day, and frightening the little mermaid so much that she had to dive under the water. She soon ventured up again, and it was just as if all the stars of heaven were falling in showers round about her. She had never seen such magic fires. Great suns whirled round, gorgeous fire-fish hung in the blue air, and all was reflected in the calm and glassy sea. It was so light on board the ship that every little rope could be seen, and the people still better. Oh! how handsome the prince was, how he laughed and smiled as he greeted his guests, while the music rang out in the quiet night.

It got quite late, but the little mermaid could not take her eyes off the ship and the beautiful prince. The coloured lanterns were put out, no more rockets were sent up, and the cannon had ceased its thunder, but deep down in the sea there was a dull murmuring and moaning sound. Meanwhile she was rocked up and down on the waves, so that she could look into the cabin; but the ship got more and more way on, sail after sail was filled by the wind, the waves grew stronger, great clouds gathered, and it lightened in the distance. Oh, there was going to be a fearful storm! and soon the sailors had to shorten sail. The great ship rocked and rolled as she dashed over the angry sea, the black waves rose like mountains, high enough to overwhelm her, but she dived like a swan through them and rose again and again on their towering crests. The little mermaid thought it a most amusing race, but not so the sailors. The ship creaked and groaned, the mighty timbers bulged and bent under the heavy blows, the water broke over the decks, snapping the main mast like a reed, she heeled over on her side and the water rushed into the hold.

Now the little mermaid saw that they were in danger and she had for her own sake to beware of the floating beams and wreckage. One moment it was so pitch dark that she could not see at all, but when the lightning flashed it became so light that she could see all on board. Every man was looking out for his own safety as best he could, but she more particularly followed the young prince with her eyes, and when the ship went down she saw him sink in the deep sea. At first she was quite delighted, for now he was coming to be with her, but then she remembered that human beings could not live under water, and that only if he were dead could he go to her father's palace. No! he must not die; so she swam towards him all among the drifting beams and planks, quite forgetting that they might crush her. She dived deep down under the water, and came up again through the waves, and at last reached the young prince just as he was becoming unable to swim any further in the stormy sea. His limbs were numbed, his beautiful eyes were closing, and he must have died if the little mermaid had not come to the rescue. She held his head above the water and let the waves drive them whithersoever they would.

By daybreak all the storm was over, of the ship not a trace was to be seen; the sun rose from the water in radiant brilliance, and his rosy beams seemed to cast a glow of life into the prince's cheeks, but his eyes remained closed. The mermaid kissed his fair and lofty brow, and stroked back the dripping hair; it seemed to her that he was like the marble statue in her little garden, she kissed him again and longed that he might live.

At last she saw dry land before her, high blue mountains on whose summits the white snow glistened as if a flock of swans had settled there; down by the shore were beautiful green woods, and in the foreground a church or temple, she did not quite know which, but it was a building of some sort. Lemon and orange trees grew in the garden and lofty palms stood by the gate. At this point the sea formed a little bay where the water was quite calm, but very deep, right up to the cliffs; at their foot was a strip of fine white sand to which she swam with the beautiful prince, and laid him down on it, taking great care that his head should rest high up in the warm sunshine. The bells now began to ring in the great white building and a number of young maidens came into the garden. Then the little mermaid swam further off behind some high rocks and covered her hair and breast with foam, so that no one should see her little face, and then she watched to see who would discover the poor prince.

It was not long before one of the maidens came up to him, at first she seemed quite frightened, but only for a moment, and then she fetched several others, and the mermaid saw that the prince was coming to life, and that he smiled at all those around him, but he never smiled at her, you see he did not know that she had saved him; she felt so sad that when he was led away into the great building she dived sorrowfully into the water and made her way home to her father's palace.

Always silent and thoughtful, she became more so now than ever. Her sisters often asked her what she had seen on her first visit to the surface, but she never would tell them anything.

Many an evening and many a morning she would rise to the place where she had left the prince. She saw the fruit in the garden ripen, and then gathered, she saw the snow melt on the mountain-tops, but she never saw the prince, so she always went home still sadder than before. At home her only consolation was to sit in her little garden with her arms twined round the handsome marble statue which reminded her of the prince. It was all in gloomy shade now, as she had ceased to tend her flowers and the garden had become a neglected wilderness of long stalks and leaves entangled with the branches of the tree.

At last she could not bear it any longer, so she told one of her sisters, and from her it soon spread to the others, but to no one else except to one or two other mermaids who only told their dearest friends. One of these knew all about the prince, she had also seen the festivities on the ship; she knew where he came from and where his kingdom was situated.

"Come, little sister!" said the other princesses, and, throwing their arms round each other's shoulders, they rose from the water in a long line, just in front of the prince's palace.

It was built of light yellow glistening stone, with great marble staircases, one of which led into the garden. Magnificent gilded cupolas rose above the roof, and the spaces between the columns which encircled the building were filled with lifelike marble statues. Through the clear glass of the lofty windows you could see gorgeous halls adorned with costly silken hangings, and the pictures on the walls were a sight worth seeing. In the midst of the central hall a large fountain played, throwing its jets of spray upwards to a glass dome in the roof, through which the sunbeams lighted up the water and the beautiful plants which grew in the great basin.

She knew now where he lived and often used to go there in the evenings and by night over the water; she swam much nearer the land than any of the others dared, she even ventured right up the narrow channel under the splendid marble terrace which threw a long shadow over the water. She used to sit here looking at the young prince who thought he was quite alone in the clear moonlight.

She saw him many an evening sailing about in his beautiful boat, with flags waving and music playing, she used to peep through the green rushes, and if the wind happened to catch her long silvery veil and any one saw it, they only thought it was a swan flapping its wings.

Many a night she heard the fishermen, who were fishing by torchlight, talking over the good deeds of the young prince; and she was happy to think that she had saved his life when he was drifting about on the waves, half dead, and she could not forget how closely his head had pressed her breast, and how passionately she had kissed him; but he knew nothing of all this, and never saw her even in his dreams.

She became fonder and fonder of mankind, and longed more and more to be able to live among them; their world seemed so infinitely bigger than hers; with their ships they could scour the ocean, they could ascend the mountains high above the clouds, and their wooded, grass-grown lands extended further than her eye could reach. There was so much that she wanted to know, but her sisters could not give an answer to all her questions, so she asked her old grandmother who knew the upper world well, and rightly called it the country above the sea. "If men are not drowned," asked the little mermaid, "do they live for ever, do they not die as we do down here in the sea?"

"Yes," said the old lady, "they have to die too, and their life time is even shorter than ours. We may live here for three hundred years, but when we cease to exist, we become mere foam on the water and do not have so much as a grave among our dear ones. We have no immortal souls, we have no future life, we are just like the green sea-weed, which, once cut down, can never revive again! Men, on the other hand, have a soul which lives for ever, lives after the body has become dust; it rises through the clear air, up to the shining stars! Just as we rise from the water to see the land of mortals, so they rise up to unknown beautiful regions which we shall never see."

"Why have we no immortal souls?" asked the little mermaid sadly. "I would give all my three hundred years to be a human being for one day, and afterwards to have a share in the heavenly kingdom."

"You must not be thinking about that," said the grand-mother, "we are much better off and happier than human beings."

"Then I shall have to die and to float as foam on the water, and never hear the music of the waves or see the beautiful flowers or the red sun! Is there nothing I can do to gain an immortal soul?"

"No," said the grandmother, "only if a human being so loved you, that you were more to him than father or mother, if all his thoughts and all his love were so centred in you that he would let the priest join your hands and would vow to be faithful to you here, and to all eternity; then your body would become infused with his soul. Thus and only thus, could you gain a share in the felicity of mankind. He would give you a soul while yet keeping his own. But that can never happen! That which is your greatest beauty in the sea, your fish's tail, is thought hideous up on earth, so little do they understand about it; to be pretty there you must have two clumsy supports which they call legs!"

Then the little mermaid sighed and looked sadly at her fish's tail.

"Let us be happy," said the grandmother, "we will hop and skip during our three hundred years of life, it is surely a long enough time, and after it is over, we shall rest all the better in our graves. There is to be a court ball to-night."

This was a much more splendid affair than we ever see on earth. The walls and the ceiling of the great ball room were of thick but transparent glass. Several hundreds of colossal mussel shells, rose-red and grass-green, were ranged in order round the sides holding blue lights, which illuminated the whole room and shone through the walls, so that the sea outside was quite lit up. You could see countless fish, great and small, swimming towards the glass walls, some with shining scales of crimson hue, while others were golden and silvery. In the middle of the room was a broad stream of running water, and on this the mermaids and mermen danced to their own beautiful singing. No earthly beings have such lovely voices. The little mermaid sang more sweetly than any of them and they all applauded her. For a moment she felt glad at heart, for she knew that she had the finest voice either in the sea or on land. But she soon began to think again about the upper world, she could not forget the handsome prince and her sorrow in not possessing, like him, an immortal soul. Therefore she stole out of her father's palace, and while all within was joy and merriment, she sat sadly in her little garden. Suddenly she heard the sound of a horn through the water, and she thought, "now he is out sailing up there; he

whom I love more than father or mother, he to whom my
thoughts cling and to whose hands I am ready to commit the
happiness of my life. I will dare anything to win him and to
gain an immortal soul! While my sisters are dancing in my
father's palace, I will go to the sea witch of whom I have
always been very much afraid, she will perhaps be able to
advise and help me!"

Thereupon the little mermaid left the garden and went
towards the roaring whirlpools at the back of which the witch
lived. She had never been that way before; no flowers grew
there, no seaweed, only the bare grey sands stretched towards
the whirlpools, which like rushing mill-wheels swirled round,
dragging everything that came within reach down to the
depths. She had to pass between these boiling eddies to reach
the witch's domain, and for a long way the only path led over
warm bubbling mud, which the witch called her "peat bog."
Her house stood behind this in the midst of a weird forest. All
the trees and bushes were polyps, half animal and half plant;
they looked like hundred-headed snakes growing out of the
sand, the branches were long slimy arms, with tentacles like
wriggling worms, every joint of which from the root to the
outermost tip was in constant motion. They wound themselves
tightly round whatever they could lay hold of and never let it
escape. The little mermaid standing outside was quite frightened, her heart beat fast with terror and she nearly turned
back, but then she remembered the prince and the immortal
soul of mankind and took courage. She bound her long flowing hair tightly round her head, so that the polyps should
not seize her by it, folded her hands over her breast, and
darted like a fish through the water, in between the hideous
polyps which stretched out their sensitive arms and tentacles

towards her. She could see that every one of them had something or other, which they had grasped with their hundred arms, and which they held as if in iron bands. The bleached bones of men who had perished at sea and sunk below peeped forth from the arms of some, while others clutched rudders and sea chests, or the skeleton of some land animal; and most horrible of all, a little mermaid whom they had caught and suffocated. Then she came to a large opening in the wood where the ground was all slimy, and where some huge fat water snakes were gambolling about. In the middle was a house built of the bones of the wrecked; there sat the witch, letting a toad eat out of her mouth, just as mortals let a little canary eat sugar. She called the hideous water snakes her little chickens, and allowed them to crawl about on her unsightly bosom.

"I know very well what you have come here for," said the witch. "It is very foolish of you! all the same you shall have your way, because it will lead you into misfortune, my fine princess. You want to get rid of your fish's tail, and instead to have two stumps to walk about upon like human beings, so that the young prince may fall in love with you, and that you may win him and an immortal soul." Saying this, she gave such a loud hideous laugh that the toad and the snakes fell to the ground and wriggled about there.

"You are just in the nick of time," said the witch, "after sunrise to-morrow I should not be able to help you until another year had run its course. I will make you a potion, and before sunrise you must swim ashore with it, seat yourself on the beach and drink it; then your tail will divide and shrivel up to what men call beautiful legs, but it hurts, it is as if a sharp sword were running through you. All who see you will say that you are the most beautiful child of man they have ever seen. You will keep your gliding gait, no dancer will rival you, but every step you take will be as if you were treading upon sharp knives, so sharp as to draw blood. If you are willing to suffer all this I am ready to help you!"

"Yes!" said the little princess with a trembling voice, thinking of the prince and of winning an undying soul.

"But remember," said the witch, "when once you have received a human form, you can never be a mermaid again, you will never again be able to dive down through the water to your sisters and to your father's palace. And if you do not succeed in winning the prince's love, so that for your sake he will forget father and mother, cleave to you with his whole heart, let the priest join your hands and make you man and wife, you will gain no immortal soul! The first morning after his marriage with another your heart will break, and you will turn into foam of the sea."

"I will do it," said the little mermaid as pale as death.

"But you will have to pay me, too," said the witch, "and it is no trifle that I demand. You have the most beautiful voice of any at the bottom of the sea, and I daresay that you think you will fascinate him with it, but you must give me that voice, I will have the best you possess in return for my precious potion! I have to mingle my own blood with it so as to make it as sharp as a two-edged sword."

"But if you take my voice," said the little mermaid, "what have I left?"

"Your beautiful form," said the witch, "your gliding gait, and your speaking eyes, with these you ought surely to be able to bewitch a human heart. Well! have you lost courage? Put out your little tongue and I will cut it off in payment for the powerful draught."

"Let it be done," said the little mermaid, and the witch put on her cauldron to brew the magic potion. "There is nothing like cleanliness," said she, as she scoured the pot with a bundle of snakes; then she punctured her breast and let the black blood drop into the cauldron, and the steam took the most weird shapes, enough to frighten any one. Every moment the witch threw new ingredients into the pot, and when it boiled the bubbling was like the sound of crocodiles weeping. At last the potion was ready and it looked like the clearest water.

"There it is," said the witch, and thereupon she cut off the tongue of the little mermaid, who was dumb now and could neither sing nor speak.

"If the polyps should seize you, when you go back through my wood," said the witch, "just drop a single drop of this liquid on them, and their arms and fingers will burst into a thousand pieces." But the little mermaid had no need to do this, for at the mere sight of the bright liquid which sparkled in her hand like a shining star, they drew back in terror. So she soon got past the wood, the bog, and the eddying whirlpools.

She saw her father's palace, the lights were all out in the great ballroom, and no doubt all the household was asleep, but she did not dare to go in now that she was dumb and about to leave her home for ever. She felt as if her heart would break with grief. She stole into the garden and plucked a flower from each of her sister's plots, wafted with her hand countless kisses towards the palace, and then rose up through the dark blue water.

The sun had not risen when she came in sight of the prince's palace and landed at the beautiful marble steps. The

moon was shining bright and clear. The little mermaid drank
the burning, stinging draught, and it was like a sharp, two-
edged sword running through her tender frame; she fainted
away and lay as if she were dead. When the sun rose on the
sea she woke up and became conscious of a sharp pang, but
just in front of her stood the handsome young prince, fixing
his coal black eyes on her; she cast hers down and saw that
her fish's tail was gone, and that she had the prettiest little
white legs any maiden could desire, but she was quite naked,
so she wrapped her long thick hair around her. The prince
asked who she was and how she came there, she looked at
him tenderly and with a sad expression in her dark blue eyes,
but could not speak. Then he took her by the hand and led
her into the palace. Every step she took was, as the witch
had warned her beforehand, as if she were treading on sharp
knives and spikes but she bore it gladly; led by the prince she
moved as lightly as a bubble, and he and every one else
marvelled at her graceful gilding gait.

Clothed in the costliest silks and muslins she was the greatest beauty in the palace, but she was dumb and could neither
sing nor speak. Beautiful slaves clad in silks and gold came
forward and sang to the prince and his royal parents; one of
them sang better than all the others, and the prince clapped
his hands and smiled at her; that made the little mermaid
very sad, for she knew that she used to sing far better herself.
She thought, "Oh! if he only knew that for the sake of being
with him I had given up my voice for ever!" Now the slaves
began to dance, graceful undulating dances to enchanting
music; thereupon the little mermaid lifting her beautiful white
arms and raising herself on tiptoe glided on the floor with a
grace which none of the other dancers had yet attained. With

every motion her grace and beauty became more apparent, and her eyes appealed more deeply to the heart than the songs of the slaves. Everyone was delighted with it, especially the prince, who called her his little foundling, and she danced on and on, notwithstanding that every time her foot touched the ground it was like treading on sharp knives. The prince said that she should always be near him, and she was allowed to sleep outside his door on a velvet cushion.

He had a man's dress made for her, so that she could ride about with him. They used to ride through scented woods, where the green branches brushed her shoulders, and little birds sang among the fresh leaves. She climbed up the highest mountains with the prince, and although her delicate feet bled so that others saw it, she only laughed and followed him until they saw the clouds sailing below them like a flock of birds, taking flight to distant lands.

At home in the prince's palace, when at night the others were asleep, she used to go out on to the marble steps; it cooled her burning feet to stand in the cold sea water, and at such times she used to think of those she had left in the deep.

One night her sisters came arm in arm; they sang so sorrowfully as they swam on the water that she beckoned to them and they recognised her, and told her how she had grieved them all. After that they visited her every night, and one night she saw, a long way out, her old grandmother (who for many years had not been above the water), and the Merman King with his crown on his head; they stretched out their hands towards her, but did not venture so close to land as her sisters.

Day by day she became dearer to the prince, he loved her as one loves a good sweet child, but it never entered his head to make her his queen; yet unless she became his wife she would

never win an everlasting soul, but on his wedding morning
would turn to sea foam.

"Am I not dearer to you than any of them?" the little
mermaid's eyes seemed to say when he took her in his arms
and kissed her beautiful brow.

"Yes, you are the dearest one to me," said the prince, "for
you have the best heart of them all, and you are fondest of
me; you are also like a young girl I once saw, but whom I
never expect to see again. I was on board a ship which was
wrecked, I was driven on shore by the waves close to a holy
Temple where several young girls were ministering at a service; the youngest of them found me on the beach and saved
my life: I saw her but twice. She was the only person I could
love in this world, but you are like her, you almost drive her
image out of my heart. She belongs to the holy Temple, and
therefore by good fortune you have been sent to me, we will
never part!"

"Alas! he does not know that it was I who saved his life,"
thought the little mermaid. "I bore him over the sea to the
wood, where the Temple stands. I sat behind the foam and
watched to see if any one would come. I saw the pretty girl
he loves better than me." And the mermaid heaved a bitter
sigh, for she could not weep.

"The girl belongs to the holy Temple, he has said, she will
never return to the world, they will never meet again, I am
here with him, I see him every day. Yes! I will tend him, love
him, and give up my life to him."

But now the rumour ran that the prince was to be married
to the beautiful daughter of a neighbouring king, and for that
reason was fitting out a splendid ship. It was given out that
the prince was going on a voyage to see the adjoining coun-

tries, but it was without doubt to see the king's daughter; he was to have a great suite with him, but the little mermaid shook her head and laughed; she knew the prince's intentions much better than any of the others. "I must take this voyage," he had said to her; "I must go and see the beautiful princess; my parents demand that, but they will never force me to bring her home as my bride; I can never love her! She will not be like the lovely girl in the Temple whom you resemble. If ever I had to choose a bride it would sooner be you with your speaking eyes, my sweet, dumb foundling!" And he kissed her rosy mouth played with her long hair, and laid his head upon her heart, which already dreamt of human joys and an immortal soul.

"You are not frightened of the sea, I suppose, my dumb child?" he said, as they stood on the proud ship which was to carry them to the country of the neighbouring king; and he told her about storms and calms, about curious fish in the deep, and the marvels seen by divers; and she smiled at his tales, for she knew all about the bottom of the sea much better than any one else.

At night, in the moonlight, when all were asleep, except the steersman at the helm, she sat at the side of the ship trying to pierce the clear water with her eyes, and fancied she saw her father's palace, and above it her old grandmother with her silver crown on her head, looking up through the cross currents towards the keel of the ship. Then her sisters rose above the water, they gazed sadly at her, wringing their white hands; she beckoned to them, smiled, and was about to tell them that all was going well and happily with her, when the cabin boy approached, and the sisters dived down, he supposed that the white objects he had seen were nothing but flakes of foam.

The next morning the ship entered the harbour of the neighbouring king's magnificent city. The church bells rang and trumpets were sounded from every lofty tower, while the soldiers paraded with flags flying and glittering bayonets. There was a *fête* every day, there was a succession of balls, and receptions followed one after the other, but the princess was not yet present, she was being brought up a long way off, in a holy Temple they said, and was learning all the royal virtues. At last she came. The little mermaid stood eager to see her beauty, and she was obliged to confess that a lovelier creature she had never beheld. Her complexion was exquisitely pure and delicate, and her trustful eyes of the deepest blue shone through their dark lashes.

"It is you," said the prince, "you who saved me when I lay almost lifeless on the beach?" and he clasped his blushing bride to his heart. "Oh! I am too happy!" he exclaimed to the little mermaid.

"A greater joy than I had dared to hope for has come to pass. You will rejoice at my joy, for you love me better than any one." Then the little mermaid kissed his hand, and felt as if her heart were broken already.

His wedding morn would bring death to her and change her to foam.

All the church bells pealed and heralds rode through the town proclaiming the nuptials. Upon every altar throughout the land fragrant oil was burnt in costly silver lamps. Amidst the swinging of censers by the priests, the bride and bridegroom joined hands and received the bishop's blessing. The little mermaid dressed in silk and gold stood holding the bride's train, but her ears were deaf to the festal strains, her eyes saw nothing of the sacred ceremony, she was thinking of her coming death and of all that she had lost in this world.

That same evening the bride and bridegroom embarked, amidst the roar of cannon and the waving of banners. A royal tent of purple and gold softly cushioned was raised amidships where the bridal pair were to repose during the calm cool night.

The sails swelled in the wind and the ship skimmed lightly and almost without motion over the transparent sea.

At dusk lanterns of many colours were lighted and the sailors danced merrily on deck. The little mermaid could not help thinking of the first time she came up from the sea and saw the same splendour and gaiety; and she now threw herself among the dancers, whirling, as a swallow skims through the air when pursued. The onlookers cheered her in amazement, never had she danced so divinely; her delicate feet pained her as if they were cut with knives, but she did not feel it, for the pain at her heart was much sharper. She knew that it was the last night that she would breathe the same air as he, and would look upon the mighty deep, and the blue starry heavens; an endless night without thought and without dreams awaited her, who neither had a soul, nor could win one. The joy and revelry on board lasted till long past midnight, she went on laughing and dancing with the thought of death all the time in her heart. The prince caressed his lovely bride and she played with his raven locks, and with their arms entwined they retired to the gorgeous tent. All became hushed and still on board the ship, only the steersman stood at the helm, the little mermaid laid her white arms on the gunwale and looked eastwards for the pink tinted dawn; the first sunbeam she knew would be her death. Then she saw her sisters rise from the water, they were as pale as she was, their beautiful long hair no longer floated on the breeze, for it had been cut off.

"We have given it to the witch to obtain her help, so that you may not die to-night! she has given us a knife, here it is, look how sharp it is! Before the sun rises, you must plunge it into the prince's heart, and when his warm blood sprinkles your feet they will join together and grow into a tail, and you will once more be a mermaid; you will be able to come down into the water to us, and to live out your three hundred years before you are turned into dead, salt, sea-foam. Make haste! you or he must die before sunrise! Our old grandmother is so full of grief that her white hair has fallen off as ours fell under the witch's scissors. Slay the prince and come back to us! Quick! Quick! do you not see the rosy streak in the sky? In a few moments the sun will rise and then you must die!" saying this they heaved a wondrous deep sigh and sank among the waves.

The little mermaid drew aside the purple curtain from the tent and looked at the beautiful bride asleep with her head on the prince's breast; she bent over him and kissed his fair brow, looked at the sky where the dawn was spreading fast; looked at the sharp knife, and again fixed her eyes on the prince who, in his dream called his bride by name, yes! she alone was in his thoughts!—For a moment the knife quivered in her grasp, then she threw it far out among the waves now rosy in the morning light and where it fell the water bubbled up like drops of blood.

Once more she looked at the prince, with her eyes already dimmed by death, then dashed overboard and fell, her body dissolving into foam.

Now the sun rose from the sea and with its kindly beams

warmed the deadly cold foam, so that the little mermaid did not feel the chill of death. She saw the bright sun and above her floated hundreds of beauteous ethereal beings through which she could see the white ship and the rosy heavens, their voices were melodious but so spirit-like that no human ear could hear them, any more than an earthly eye could see their forms. Light as bubbles they floated through the air without the aid of wings. The little mermaid perceived that she had a form like theirs, it gradually took shape out of the foam. "To whom am I coming?" said she, and her voice sounded like that of the other beings, so unearthly in its beauty that no music of ours could reproduce it.

"To the daughters of the air!" answered the others, "a mermaid has no undying soul, and can never gain one without winning the love of a human being. Her eternal life must depend upon an unknown power. Nor have the daughters of the air an everlasting soul, but by their own good deeds they may create one for themselves. We fly to the tropics where mankind is the victim of hot and pestilent winds, there we bring cooling breezes. We diffuse the scent of flowers all around, and bring refreshment and healing in our train. When, for three hundred years, we have laboured to do all the good in our power we gain an undying soul and take a part in the everlasting joys of mankind. You, poor little mermaid, have with your whole heart struggled for the same thing, as we have struggled for. You have suffered and endured, raised yourself to the spirit world of the air; and now, by your own good deeds you may, in the course of three hundred years, work out for yourself an undying soul."

Then the little mermaid lifted her transparent arms towards God's sun, and for the first time shed tears.

On board ship all was again life and bustle, she saw the prince with his lovely bride searching for her, they looked sadly at the bubbling foam, as if they knew that she had thrown herself into the waves. Unseen she kissed the bride on her brow, smiled at the prince and rose aloft with the other spirits of the air to the rosy clouds which sailed above.

"In three hundred years we shall thus float into Paradise."

"We might reach it sooner," whispered one. "Unseen we flit into those homes of men where there are children, and for every day that we find a good child who gives pleasure to its parents and deserves their love, God shortens our time of probation. The child does not know when we fly through the room, and when we smile with pleasure at it, one year of our three hundred is taken away. But if we see a naughty or badly disposed child, we cannot help shedding tears of sorrow, and every tear adds a day to the time of our probation."

The Flying Trunk

There was once a merchant who was so rich that he might have paved the whole street, and a little alley besides, with silver money. But he didn't do it—he knew better how to use his money than that: if he laid out a penny, he got half a crown in return, such a clever man of business was he—and then he died.

His son got all the money, and he led a merry life; he used to go to masquerades every night, made kites of bank notes, and played ducks and drakes with gold coins instead of stones. In this way the money soon went. At last he had only a penny left, and no clothes except an old dressing-gown and a pair of slippers. His friends cared for him no longer, they couldn't walk about the streets with him; but one of them who was kind sent him an old trunk, and said, "Pack up." Now this was all very well, but he had nothing to pack, so he got into the trunk himself.

It was a most peculiar trunk. If you pressed the lock the trunk could fly; and this is what happened: with a whiz it flew up the chimney, high above the clouds, further and further away. The bottom of it cracked ominously, and he was dreadfully afraid it would go to pieces, and a nice fall he would have had! Heaven preserve us! At last he arrived in the country of the Turks. He hid the trunk in a wood under the dead leaves, and walked into the town; he could easily do that, as all the Turks wear dressing-gowns and slippers, you know, just like his. He met a nurse with a baby. "I say, you Turkish nurse", said he, "what is that big palace close to the town, where all the windows are so high up?"

"That's where the king's daughter lives," said she; "it has been prophesied that she will be made very unhappy by a lover, so no one is allowed to visit her except when the king and the queen go with them."

"Thank you," said the merchant's son, and then he went back to the wood and got into his trunk again, and flew on to the roof of the palace, from whence he crept in at the princess's window.

She was lying on a sofa, fast asleep. She was so very beautiful that the merchant's son was driven to kiss her. She woke up and was dreadfully frightened, but he said that he was the Prophet of the Turks and he had flown down through the air to see her, and this pleased her very much.

They sat side by side and he told her stories about her eyes; he said they were like the most beautiful deep, dark lakes, in which her thoughts floated like mermaids; and then he told her about her forehead, that it was like a snow mountain, adorned with a series of pictures. And he told her all about the storks, which bring beautiful little children up out of the rivers. No end of beautiful stories he told her, and then he asked her to marry him, and she at once said "Yes." "But you must come here on Saturday," she said, "when the king and the queen drink tea with me. They will be very proud when they hear I am to marry a prophet; but mind you have a splendid story to tell them, for my parents are very fond of stories: my mother likes them to be grand and very proper, but my father likes them to be merry, so that he can laugh at them."

"Well, a story will be my only wedding-gift!" he said, and then they separated: but the princess gave him a sword encrusted with gold. It was the kind of present he needed badly.

He flew away and bought himself a new dressing-gown, and sat down in the wood to make up a new story; it had to be ready by Saturday, and it is not always so easy to make up a story.

However he had it ready in time, and Saturday came.

The king, the queen and the whole court were waiting for him round the princess's tea-table. He had a charming reception.

"Now will you tell us a story," said the queen, "one which is both thoughtful and instructive."

"But one that we can laugh at too," said the king.

"All right!" said he, and then he began: we must listen to his story attentively.

"There was once a bundle of matches, and they were frightfully proud because of their high origin. Their family tree, that is to say the great pine tree of which they were each a little splinter, had been the giant of the forest. The matches now lay on a shelf between a tinder-box and an old iron pot, and they told the whole story of their youth to these two. 'Ah, when we were a living tree,' said they, 'we were indeed a green branch! Every morning and every evening we had diamond-tea, that was the dew-drops. In the day we had the sunshine, and all the little birds to tell us stories. We could see, too, that we were very rich, for most of the other trees were only clad in summer, but our family could afford to have green clothes both summer and winter. But then the wood-cutters came, and there was a great revolution, and our family was sundered. The head of the tribe got a place as mainmast on a splendid ship, which could sail round the world if it chose; the other branches were scattered in different directions, and it is now our task to give light to the common herd, that is how such aristocratic people as ourselves have got into this kitchen.'

" 'Now my lot has been different!' said the iron pot, beside which the matches lay. 'Ever since I came into the world I have passed the time in being scoured and boiled, over and over again! Everything solid comes to me, and in fact I am the most important person in the house. My pleasure is when the dinner is over, to lie clean and bright on the shelf, and to have a sensible chat with my companions; but with the exception of the water-bucket, which sometimes goes down into the yard, we lead an indoor life. Our only newsmonger is the market-basket, and it talks very wildly about the Government and the People. Why the other day an old pot was so alarmed by the conversation, that it fell down and broke itself to pieces! It was a Liberal you see!'

" 'You are talking too much,' said the tinder-box, and the steel struck sparks on the flint. 'Let us have a merry evening.'

" 'Yes, pray let us settle which is the most aristocratic among us,' said the matches.

" 'No, I don't like talking about myself,' said the earthen pipkin; 'let us have an evening entertainment! I will begin. I will tell you the kind of things we have all experienced; they are quite easy to understand, and that is what we all like: By the eastern sea and Danish beeches—'

" 'That's a nice beginning to make!' said all the plates; 'I am sure that will be a story I shall like!'

" 'Well, I passed my youth there in, a very quiet family; the furniture was bees-waxed, the floors washed, and clean curtains were put up once a fortnight!'

" 'What a good story-teller you are,' said the broom; 'one can tell directly that it's a woman telling a story, a vein of cleanliness runs through it!'

" 'Yes, one feels that,' said the water-pail, and for very joy it gave a little hop which clashed on the floor.

"The pipkin went on with its story, and the end was much the same as the beginning.

"All the plates clattered with joy, and the broom crowned the pipkin with a wreath of parsley, because it knew it would annoy the others; and it thought, 'If I crown her to-day, she will crown me to-morrow.'

" 'Now I will dance' said the tongs, and began to dance; heaven help us, what a way into the air she could get her leg. The old chair-cover in the corner burst when she saw it!

'Mayn't I be crowned too,' said the tongs, so they crowned her. " 'They're only a rabble after all,' said the matches.

"The tea-urn was called upon to sing now, but it had a cold, it said; it couldn't sing except when it was boiling; but that was all because it was stuck-up; it *wouldn't* sing except when it was on the drawing-room table.

"There was an old quill pen, along on the window-sill, which the servant used to write with; there was nothing extraordinary about it, except that it had been dipped too far into the inkpot, but it was rather proud of that. 'If the tea-urn won't sing, it can leave it alone,' it said. 'There is a nightingale hanging outside in a cage, it can sing; it certainly hasn't learnt anything special, but we needn't mind that to-night.'

" 'I think it is most unsuitable,' said the kettle, which was the kitchen songster, and half-sister of the urn, 'that a strange bird like that should be listened to! Is it patriotic? I will let the market-basket judge.'

" 'I am very much annoyed,' said the market-basket. 'I am more annoyed than any one can tell! Is this a suitable way to spend an evening? Wouldn't it be better to put the house to rights? Then everything would find its proper place, and I would manage the whole party. Then we should get on differently!'

" 'Yes, let us make a row!' they all said together.

"At that moment the door opened, it was the servant, and they all stood still, nobody uttered a sound. But not a pot among them which didn't know its capabilities, or how distinguished it was, 'If *I* had chosen, we might have had a merry evening, and no mistake,' they all thought.

"The servant took the matches and struck a light; preserve us! how they spluttered and blazed up.

" 'Now everyone can see,' they thought, 'that we are the first. How brilliantly we shine! What a light we shed around!' —And then they were burnt out."

"That was a splendid story," said the queen; "I quite felt that I was in the kitchen with the matches. Yes indeed you shall marry our daughter."

"Certainly!" said the king. "Thou shalt marry her on Monday!" They said "du" (thou) to him now, as they were to be related.

So the wedding was decided upon, and the evening before the town was illuminated. Buns and cakes were scattered broadcast; the street boys stood on tiptoe and shouted hurrah, and whistled through their fingers. Everything was most gorgeous.

"I suppose I shall have to do something too," said the merchant's son; so he bought a lot of rockets, squibs, and all sorts of fireworks, put them in his trunk, and flew up into the air with them.

All the Turks jumped at the sight, so that their slippers flew up into the air, they had never seen a flight of meteors like that before. They saw now without doubt that it was the prophet himself, who was about to marry the princess.

As soon as the merchant's son got down again into the wood with his trunk, he thought, "I will just go into the town to hear what was thought of the display," and it was quite reasonable that he should do so.

Oh, how every one talked, every single man he spoke to had his own opinion about it, but that it had been splendid was the universal opinion.

"I saw the prophet myself," said one; "his eyes were like shining stars, and his beard like foaming water."

"He was wrapped in a mantle of fire," said another. "The most beautiful angels' heads peeped out among the folds." He heard nothing but pleasant things and the next day was to be his wedding-day. He went back to the wood to get into his trunk—but where was it? The trunk was burnt up. A spark from the fireworks had set fire to it and the trunk was burnt to ashes. He could not fly any more, or reach his bride. She stood all day on the roof waiting for him; she is waiting for him still, but he wanders round the world telling stories, only they are no longer so merry as the one he told about the matches.

The Real Princess

There was once a prince, and he wanted a princess, but then she must be a *real* princess. He travelled right round the world to find one, but there was always something wrong. There were plenty of princesses, but whether they were real princesses he had great difficulty in discovering; there was always something which was not quite right about them. So at last he had to come home again, and he was very sad because he wanted a real princess so badly.

One evening there was a terrible storm; it thundered and lightened and the rain poured down in torrents; indeed it was a fearful night.

In the middle of the storm somebody knocked at the town gate, and the old king himself went to open it.

It was a princess who stood outside, but she was in a terrible state from the rain and the storm. The water streamed out of her hair and her clothes, it ran in at the top of her shoes and out at the heel, but she said that she was a real princess.

"Well we shall soon see if that is true," thought the old queen, but she said nothing. She went into the bedroom, took all the bedclothes off and laid a pea on the bedstead: then she took twenty mattresses and piled them on the top of the pea, and then twenty feather beds on the top of the mattresses. This was where the princess was to sleep that night. In the morning they asked her how she had slept.

"Oh terribly badly!" said the Princess. "I have hardly closed my eyes the whole night! Heaven knows what was in the bed. I seemed to be lying upon some hard thing, and my whole body is black and blue this morning. It is terrible!"

They saw at once that she must be a real princess when she had felt the pea through twenty mattresses and twenty feather beds. Nobody but a real princess could have such a delicate skin.

So the prince took her to be his wife, for now he was sure that he had found a real princess, and the pea was put into the Museum, where it may still be seen if no one has stolen it.

Now this is a true story.

The Red Shoes

There was once a little girl; she was a tiny, delicate little thing, but she always had to go about barefoot in summer, because she was very poor. In winter she only had a pair of heavy wooden shoes, and her ankles were terribly chafed.

An old mother shoemaker lived in the middle of the village, and she made a pair of little shoes out of some strips of red cloth. They were very clumsy, but they were made with the best intention, for the little girl was to have them. Her name was Karen.

These shoes were given to her, and she wore them for the first time on the day her mother was buried; they were certainly not mourning, but she had no others, and so she walked barelegged in them behind the poor deal coffin.

Just then a big old carriage drove by, and a big old lady was seated in it; she looked at the little girl and felt very very sorry for her, and said to the Parson, "Give the little girl to me and I will look after her and be kind to her." Karen thought it was all because of the red shoes, but the old lady said they were hideous, and they were burnt. Karen was well and neatly dressed, and had to learn reading and sewing. People said she was pretty, but her mirror said, "you are more than pretty, you are lovely."

At this time the queen was taking a journey through the country, and she had her little daughter the princess with her. The people, and among them Karen, crowded round the

palace where they were staying, to see them. The little princess stood at a window to show herself. She wore neither a
train nor a golden crown, but she was dressed all in white
with a beautiful pair of red morocco shoes. They were indeed
a contrast to those the poor old mother shoemaker had made
for Karen. Nothing in the world could be compared to these
red shoes.

The time came when Karen was old enough to be confirmed; she had new clothes, and she was also to have a pair of new shoes. The rich shoemaker in the town was to take the measure of her little foot; his shop was full of glass cases of the most charming shoes and shiny leather boots. They looked beautiful, but the old lady could not see very well, so it gave her no pleasure to look at them. Among all the other shoes there was one pair of red shoes like those worn by the princess; oh, how pretty they were. The shoemaker told them that they had been made for an earl's daughter, but they had not fitted. "I suppose they are patent leather," said the old lady, "they are so shiny."

"Yes, they do shine," said Karen, who tried them on. They fitted and were bought; but the old lady had not the least idea that they were red, or she would never have allowed Karen to wear them for her Confirmation. This she did however.

Everybody looked at her feet, and when she walked up the church to the chancel, she thought that even the old pictures, those portraits of dead and gone priests and their wives, with stiff collars and long black clothes, fixed their eyes upon her shoes. She thought of nothing else when the priest laid his hand upon her head and spoke to her of holy baptism, the covenant of God, and that from henceforth she was to be a responsible Christian person. The solemn notes of the organ resounded, the children sang with their sweet voices, the old precentor sang, but Karen only thought about her red shoes.

By the afternoon the old lady had been told on all sides that the shoes were red, and she said it was very naughty and most improper. For the future, whenever Karen went to the church, she was to wear black shoes, even if they were old. Next Sunday there was Holy Communion, and Karen was

to receive it for the first time. She looked at the black shoes
and then at the red ones—then she looked again at the red,
and at last put them on.

It was beautiful, sunny weather; Karen and the old lady
went by the path through the cornfield, and it was rather
dusty. By the church door stood an old soldier, with a crutch;
he had a curious long beard, it was more red than white, in
fact it was almost quite red. He bent down to the ground
and asked the old lady if he might dust her shoes. Karen put out
her little foot too. "See, what beautiful dancing shoes!" said
the soldier. "Mind you stick fast when you dance," and as he
spoke he struck the soles with his hand. The old lady gave
the soldier a copper and went into the church with Karen.
All the people in the church looked at Karen's red shoes, and
all the portraits looked too. When Karen knelt at the altar-
rails and the chalice was put to her lips, she only thought of
the red shoes; she seemed to see them floating before her
eyes. She forgot to join in the hymn of praise, and she forgot
to say the Lord's Prayer.

Now everybody left the church, and the old lady got into
her carriage. Karen lifted her foot to get in after her, but just
then the old soldier, who was still standing there, said, "See
what pretty dancing shoes!" Karen couldn't help it; she took
a few dancing steps, and when she began her feet continued to
dance; it was just as if the shoes had a power over them. She
danced right round the church; she couldn't stop; the coachman had to run after her and take hold of her, and lift her
into the carriage; but her feet continued to dance, so that she
kicked the poor lady horribly. At last they got the shoes off,
and her feet had a little rest.

When they got home the shoes were put away in a

cupboard, but Karen could not help going to look at them.

The old lady became very ill; they said she could not live; she had to be carefully nursed and tended, and no one was nearer than Karen to do this. But there was to be a grand ball in the town, and Karen was invited. She looked at the old lady, who after all could not live; she looked at the red shoes; she thought there was no harm in doing so. She put on the red shoes, even that she might do; but then she went to the ball and began to dance! The shoes would not let her do what she liked: when she wanted to go to the right, they danced to the left: when she wanted to dance up the room, the shoes danced down the room, then down the stairs, through the streets and out of the town gate. Away she danced, and away she had to dance, right away into the dark forest. Something shone up above the trees, and she thought it was the moon, for it was a face, but it was the old soldier with the red beard, and he nodded and said, "See what pretty dancing shoes!"

This frightened her terribly and she wanted to throw off the red shoes, but they stuck fast. She tore off her stockings, but the shoes had grown fast to her feet, and off she danced, and off she had to dance over fields and meadows, in rain and sunshine, by day and by night, but at night it was fearful.

She danced into the open churchyard, but the dead did not join her dance, they had something better to do. She wanted to sit down on a pauper's grave where the bitter wormwood grew, but there was no rest nor repose for her. When she danced towards the open church door, she saw an angel standing there in long white robes and wings which reached from his shoulders to the ground, his face was grave and stern, and in his hand he held a broad and shining sword.

"Dance you shall!" said he, "you shall dance in your red shoes till you are pale and cold. Till your skin shrivels up and you are a skeleton! You shall dance from door to door, and wherever you find proud vain children, you must knock at the door so that they may see you and fear you. Yea, you shall dance——"

"Mercy!" shrieked Karen, but she did not hear the angel's answer, for the shoes bore her through the gate into the fields over roadways and paths, ever and ever she was forced to dance.

One morning she danced past a door she knew well; she heard the sound of a hymn from within, and a coffin covered with flowers was being carried out. Then she knew that the old lady was dead, and it seemed to her that she was forsaken by all the world, and cursed by the holy angels of God.

On and ever on she danced; dance she must even through the dark nights. The shoes bore her away over briars and stubble till her feet were torn and bleeding; she danced away over the heath till she came to a little lonely house. She knew the executioner lived here, and she tapped with her fingers on the window pane and said,—

"Come out! come out! I can't come in for I am dancing!"

The executioner said, "You can't know who I am? I chop the bad people's heads off, and I see that my axe is quivering."

"Don't chop my head off," said Karen, "for then I can never repent of my sins, but pray, pray chop my feet off with the red shoes!"

Then she confessed all her sins, and the executioner chopped off her feet with the red shoes, but the shoes danced right away with the little feet into the depths of the forest.

Then he made her a pair of wooden legs and crutches, and

he taught her a psalm, the one penitents always sing; and she kissed the hand which had wielded the axe, and went away over the heath.

"I have suffered enough for those red shoes!" said she. "I will go to church now, so that they may see me!" and she went as fast as she could to the church door. When she got there, the red shoes danced up in front of her, and she was frightened and went home again.

She was very sad all the week, and shed many bitter tears, but when Sunday came, she said, "Now then, I have suffered and struggled long enough; I should think I am quite as good as many who sit holding their heads so high in church!" She went along quite boldly, but she did not get further than the gate before she saw the red shoes dancing in front of her; she was more frightened than ever, and turned back, this time with real repentance in her heart. Then she went to the parson's house, and begged to be taken into service, she would be very industrious and work as hard as she could, she didn't care what wages they gave her, if only she might have a roof over her head and live among kind people. The parson's wife was sorry for her, and took her into her service; she proved to be very industrious and thoughtful. She sat very still, and listened most attentively in the evening when the parson read the Bible. All the little ones were very fond of her, but when they chattered about finery and dress, and about being as beautiful as a queen, she would shake her head.

Next Sunday they all went to church, and they asked her if she would go with them; but she looked sadly, with tears in her eyes, at her crutches, and they went without her to hear the word of God, and she sat in her little room alone. It was only big enough for a bed and a chair; she sat there with her prayerbook in her hand, and as she read it with a humble mind, she heard the notes of the organ, borne from the church by the wind; she raised her tear-stained face and said, "Oh, God help me!"

Then the sun shone brightly round her, and the angel in the white robes whom she had seen on yonder night, at the church door, stood before her. He no longer held the sharp sword in his hand, but a beautiful green branch, covered with roses. He touched the ceiling with it and it rose to a great height, and wherever he touched it a golden star appeared. Then he touched the walls and they spread themselves out, and she saw and heard the organ. She saw the pictures of the old parsons and their wives; the congregation were all sitting in their seats singing aloud—for the church itself had come home to the poor girl, in her narrow little chamber, or else she had been taken to it. She found herself on the bench with the other people from the Parsonage. And when the hymn had come to an end they looked up and nodded to her and said, "it was a good thing you came after all, little Karen!"

"It was through God's mercy!" she said. The organ sounded, and the children's voices echoed so sweetly through the choir. The warm sunshine streamed brightly in through the window, right up to the bench where Karen sat; her heart was so over-filled with the sunshine, with peace, and with joy, that it broke. Her soul flew with the sunshine to heaven, and no one there asked about the red shoes.

The Nightingale

In China, as you know, the Emperor is a Chinaman, and all the people around him are Chinamen too. It is many years since the story I am going to tell you happened, but that is all the more reason for telling it, lest it should be forgotten. The emperor's palace was the most beautiful thing in the world; it was made entirely of the finest porcelain, very costly, but at the same time so fragile that it could only be touched with the very greatest care. There were the most extraordinary flowers to be seen in the garden; the most beautiful ones had little silver bells tied to them, which tinkled perpetually, so that one should not pass the flowers without looking at them. Every little detail in the garden had been most carefully thought out, and it was so big, that even the gardener himself did not know where it ended. If one went on walking, one came to beautiful woods with lofty trees and deep lakes. The wood extended to the sea, which was deep and blue, deep enough for large ships to sail up right under the branches of the trees. Among these trees lived a nightingale which sang so deliciously, that even the poor fisherman who had plenty of other things to do, lay still to listen to it, when he was out at night drawing in his nets. "Heavens, how beautiful it is!" he said, but then he had to attend to his business and forgot it. The next night when he heard it again he would again exclaim, "Heavens, how beautiful it is!"

Travellers came to the emperor's capital, from every country in the world; they admired everything very much, especially the palace and the gardens, but when they heard the nightingale they all said, "This is better than anything!"

When they got home they described it, and the learned ones wrote many books about the town, the palace, and the garden, but nobody forgot the nightingale, it was always put above everything else. Those among them who were poets wrote the most beautiful poems, all about the nightingale in the woods by the deep blue sea. These books went all over the world, and in course of time some of them reached the emperor. He sat in his golden chair reading and reading, and nodding his head, well pleased to hear such beautiful descriptions of the town, the palace, and the garden. "But the nightingale is the best of all," he read.

"What is this?" said the emperor. "The nightingale? Why I know nothing about it. Is there such a bird in my kingdom, and in my own garden into the bargain, and I have never heard of it? Imagine my having to discover this from a book?"

Then he called his gentleman-in-waiting, who was so grand that when anyone of a lower rank dared to speak to him, or to ask him a question, he only would answer "P", which means nothing at all.

"There is said to be a very wonderful bird called a nightingale here," said the emperor. "They say that it is better than anything else in all my great kingdom! Why have I never been told anything about it?"

"I have never heard it mentioned," said the gentleman-in-waiting. "It has never been presented at court."

"I wish it to appear here this evening to sing to me," said the emperor. "The whole world knows what I am possessed of, and I know nothing about it!"

"I have never heard it mentioned before," said the gentleman-in-waiting. "I will seek it, and I will find it!" But where was it to be found? The gentleman-in-waiting ran upstairs and downstairs and in and out of all the rooms and corridors. No one of all those he met had ever heard anything about the nightingale; so the gentleman-in-waiting ran back to the emperor, and said that it must be a myth, invented by the writers of the books. "Your imperial majesty must not believe everything that is written; books are often mere inventions, even if they do not belong to what we call the black art!"

"But the book in which I read it is sent to me by the powerful Emperor of Japan, so it can't be untrue, I will hear this nightingale, I insist upon its being here to-night. I extend my most gracious protection to it, and if it is not forthcoming, I will have the whole court trampled upon after supper!"

"Tsing-pe" said the gentleman-in-waiting, and away he ran again, up and down all the stairs, in and out of all the rooms and corridors; half the court ran with him, for they none of them wished to be trampled on. There was much questioning about this nightingale, which was known to all the outside world, but to no one at court. At last they found a poor little maid in the kitchen. She said, "Oh heavens, the nightingale? I know it very well. Yes, indeed it can sing. Every evening I am allowed to take broken meat to my poor sick mother: she lives down by the shore. On my way back when I am tired, I rest awhile in the wood, and then I hear the nightingale. Its song brings the tears into my eyes, I feel as if my mother were kissing me!"

"Little kitchen-maid," said the gentleman-in-waiting, "I will procure you a permanent position in the kitchen and permission to see the emperor dining, if you will take us to

the nightingale. It is commanded to appear at court to-night."

Then they all went out into the wood where the nightingale usually sang. Half the court was there. As they were going along at their best pace a cow began to bellow.

"O!" said a young courtier, "there we have it. What wonderful power for such a little creature; I have certainly heard it before."

"No, those are the cows bellowing, we are a long way yet from the place." Then the frogs began to croak in the marsh.

"Beautiful?" said the Chinese chaplain, "it is just like the tinkling of church bells."

"No, those are the frogs!" said the little kitchen-maid. "But I think we shall soon hear it now!"

Then the nightingale began to sing.

"There it is!" said the little girl. "Listen, listen, there it sits!" and she pointed to a little grey bird up among the branches.

"Is it possible?" said the gentleman-in-waiting. "I should never have thought it was like that. How common it looks. Seeing so many grand people must have frightened all its colours away."

"Little nightingale!" called the kitchen maid quite loud, "our gracious emperor wishes you to sing to him!"

"With the greatest pleasure!" said the nightingale, warbling away in the most delightful fashion.

"It is just like crystal bells," said the gentleman-in-waiting. "Look at its little throat, how active it is. It is extraordinary that we have never heard it before! I am sure it will be a great success at court!"

"Shall I sing again to the emperor?" said the nightingale, who thought he was present.

"My precious little nightingale," said the gentleman-in-waiting, "I have the honour to command your attendance at a court festival to-night, where you will charm his gracious majesty the emperor with your fascinating singing."

"It sounds best among the trees," said the nightingale, but it went with them willingly when it heard that the emperor wished it.

The palace had been brightened up for the occasion. The walls and the floors which were all of china shone by the light of many thousand golden lamps. The most beautiful flowers, all of the tinkling kind, were arranged in the corridors; there was hurrying to and fro, and a great draught, but this was just what made the bells ring, one's ears were full of the tinkling. In the middle of the large reception-room where the emperor sat, a golden rod had been fixed, on which the nightingale was to perch. The whole court was assembled, and the little kitchenmaid had been permitted to stand behind the door, as she now had the actual title of cook. They were all dressed in their best; everybody's eyes were turned towards the little grey bird at which the emperor was nodding. The nightingale sang delightfully, and the tears came into the emperor's eyes, nay, they rolled down his cheeks, and then the nightingale sang more beautifully than ever, its notes touched all hearts. The emperor was charmed, and said the nightingale should have his gold slipper to wear round its neck. But the nightingale declined with thanks, it had already been sufficiently rewarded.

"I have seen tears in the eyes of the emperor, that is my richest reward. The tears of an emperor have a wonderful power! God knows I am sufficiently recompensed!" and then it again burst into its sweet heavenly song.

"That is the most delightful coquetting I have ever seen!" said the ladies, and they took some water into their mouths to try and make the same gurgling, when anyone spoke to them, thinking so to equal the nightingale. Even the lackeys and the chambermaids announced that they were satisfied, and that is saying a great deal, they are always the most difficult people to please. Yes, indeed, the nightingale had made a sensation. It was to stay at court now, and to have its own cage, as well as liberty to walk out twice a day, and once in the night. It always had twelve footmen with each one holding a ribbon which was tied round its leg. There was not much pleasure in an outing of that sort.

The whole town talked about the marvellous bird, and if two people met, one said to the other "Night," and the other answered "Gale," and then they sighed, perfectly understanding each other. Eleven cheesemongers' children were called after it, but they had not got a voice among them.

One day a large parcel came for the emperor, outside was written the word "Nightingale."

"Here we have another new book about this celebrated bird," said the emperor. But it was no book, it was a little work of art in a box, an artificial nightingale, exactly like the living one, but it was studded all over with diamonds, rubies, and sapphires. When the bird was wound up, it could sing one of the songs the real one sang, and it wagged its tail which glittered with silver and gold. A ribbon was tied round its neck on which was written, "The Emperor of Japan's nightingale is very poor compared to the Emperor of China's."

Everybody said, "Oh, how beautiful!" And the person who brought the artificial bird immediately received the title of Imperial Nightingale-Carrier-in-Chief.

"Now, they must sing together; what a duet that will be."

Then they had to sing together, but they did not get on very well, for the real nightingale sang in its own way, and the artificial one could only sing waltzes.

"There is no fault in that," said the music master; "it is perfectly in time and correct in every way!"

Then the artificial bird had to sing alone. It was just as great a success as the real one, and then it was so much prettier to look at, it glittered like bracelets and breast-pins.

It sang the same tune three and thirty times over, and yet it was not tired; people would willingly have heard it from the beginning again, but the Emperor said that the real one must have a turn now—but where was it? No one had noticed that it had flown out of the open window, back its to own green woods.

"But what is the meaning of this?" said the emperor.

All the courtiers railed at it, and said it was a most ungrateful bird.

"We have got the best bird though," said they, and then the artificial bird had to sing again, and this was the thirty-fourth time that they heard the same tune, but they did not know it thoroughly even yet, because it was so difficult.

The music master praised the bird tremendously, and insisted that it was much better than the real nightingale, not only as regarded the outside with all the diamonds, but the inside too.

"Because you see, my ladies and gentlemen, and the emperor before all, in the real nightingale you never know what you will hear, but in the artificial one everything is decided beforehand! So it is, and so it must remain, it can't be otherwise. You can account for things, you can open it and show

the human ingenuity in arranging the waltzes, how they go, and how one note follows upon another!"

"Those are exactly my opinions," they all said, and the music master got leave to show the bird to the public next Sunday. They were also to hear it sing, said the emperor. So they heard it, and all became as enthusiastic over it as if they had drunk themselves merry on tea, because that is a thoroughly Chinese habit.

Then they all said "Oh," and stuck their forefingers in the air and nodded their heads; but the poor fishermen who had heard the real nightingale said, "It sounds very nice, and it is very like the real one, but there is something wanting, we don't know what." The real nightingale was banished from the kingdom.

The artificial bird had its place on a silken cushion, close to the emperor's bed: all the presents it had received of gold and precious jewels were scattered round it. Its title had risen to be "Chief Imperial Singer of the Bed-Chamber," in rank number one, on the left side; for the emperor reckoned that side the important one, where the heart was seated. And even an emperor's heart is on the left side.

The music master wrote five and twenty volumes about the artificial bird; the treatise was very long, and written in all the most difficult Chinese characters. Everybody said they had read and understood it, for otherwise they would have been reckoned stupid, and then their bodies would have been trampled upon.

Things went on in this way for a whole year. The emperor, the court, and all the other Chinamen knew every little gurgle in the song of the artificial bird by heart; but they liked it all the better for this, and they could all join in the song themselves. Even the street boys sang "zizizi" and "cluck, cluck, cluck," and the emperor sang it too.

But one evening when the bird was singing its best, and the emperor was lying in bed listening to it, something gave way inside the bird with a "whizz." Then a spring burst, "whirr" went all the wheels and the music stopped. The emperor jumped out of bed and sent for his private physicians, but what good could they do? Then they sent for the watchmaker, and after a good deal of talk and examination, he got the works to go again somehow; but he said it would have to be saved as much as possible, because it was so worn out, and he could not renew the works so as to be sure of the tune. This was a great blow! They only dared to let the artificial bird sing once a year, and hardly that; but then the music master made a little speech using all the most difficult words. He said it was just as good as ever, and his saying it made it so.

Five years now passed, and then a great grief came upon the nation, for they were all very fond of their emperor, and he was ill and could not live, it was said. A new emperor was already chosen, and people stood about in the street, and asked the gentleman-in-waiting how their emperor was going on.

"P," answered he, shaking his head.

The emperor lay pale and cold in his gorgeous bed, the courtiers thought he was dead, and they all went off to pay their respects to their new emperor. The lackeys ran off to talk matters over, and the chambermaids gave a great coffee party. Cloth had been laid down in all the rooms and corridors so as to deaden the sound of footsteps, so it was very, very quiet. But the emperor was not dead yet. He lay stiff and pale in the gorgeous bed with its velvet hangings and heavy golden tassels. There was an open window high above him, and the moon streamed in upon the emperor, and the artificial bird beside him.

The poor emperor could hardly breathe, he seemed to have a weight on his chest, he opened his eyes and then he saw that it was Death sitting upon his chest, wearing his golden crown. In one hand he held the emperor's golden sword, and in the other his imperial banner. Round about, from among the folds of the velvet hangings peered many curious faces, some were hideous, others gentle and pleasant. They were all the emperor's good and bad deeds, which now looked him in the face when Death was weighing him down.

"Do you remember that?" whispered one after the other, "Do you remember this?" and they told him so many things that the perspiration poured down his face.

"I never knew that," said the emperor. "Music, music, sound the great Chinese drums!" he cried, "that I may not hear what they are saying." But they went on and on, and Death sat nodding his head, just like a Chinaman, at everything that was said.

"Music, music!" shrieked the emperor. "You precious little golden bird, sing, sing! I have loaded you with precious stones, and even hung my own golden slipper round your neck, sing, I tell you, sing!"

But the bird stood silent, there was nobody to wind it up, so of course it could not go. Death continued to fix the great empty sockets of its eyes upon him, and all was silent, so terribly silent.

Suddenly, close to the window, there was a burst of lovely song; it was the living nightingale, perched on a branch out-side. It had heard of the emperor's need, and had come to bring comfort and hope to him. As it sang the faces round became fainter and fainter, and the blood coursed with fresh vigour in the emperor's veins and through his feeble limbs. Even Death himself listened to the song and said, "Go on little nightingale, go on!"

"Yes, if you give me the gorgeous golden sword; yes, if you give me the imperial banner; yes, if you give me the emperor's crown."

And Death gave back each of these treasures for a song, and the nightingale went on singing. It sang about the quiet churchyard, where the roses bloom, where the elder flowers scent the air, and where the fresh grass is ever moistened anew by the tears of the mourner. This song brought to Death a longing for his own garden, and like a cold grey mist, he passed out of the window.

"Thanks, thanks!" said the emperor: "you heavenly little bird, I know you! I banished you from my kingdom, and yet you have charmed the evil visions away from my bed by your song, and even Death away from my heart! How can I ever repay you?"

"You have rewarded me," said the nightingale. "I brought the tears to your eyes the very first time I ever sang to you, and I shall never forget it! Those are the jewels which gladden the heart of a singer; but sleep now, and wake up fresh and strong; I will sing to you!"

Then it sang again, and the emperor fell into a sweet refreshing sleep. The sun shone in at his window, when he woke refreshed and well; none of his attendants had yet come back to him, for they thought he was dead, but the nightingale still sat there singing.

"You must always stay with me!" said the emperor. "You

shall only sing when you like, and I will break the artificial bird into a thousand pieces!"

"Don't do that!" said the nightingale, "it did all the good it could! keep it as you have always done! I can't build my nest and live in this palace, but let me come whenever I like, then I will sit on the branch in the evening, and sing to you. I will sing to cheer you and to make you thoughtful too. I will sing to you of the happy ones, and of those that suffer too. I will sing about the good and the evil, which are kept hidden from you. The little singing bird flies far and wide, to the poor fisherman, and the peasant's home, to numbers who are far from you and your court. I love your heart more than your crown, and yet there is an odour of sanctity round the crown too!—I will come, and I will sing to you!—But you must promise me one thing!"—

"Everything!" said the emperor, who stood there in his imperial robes which he had just put on, and he held the sword heavy with gold upon his heart.

"One thing I ask you! Tell no one that you have a little bird who tells you everything, it will be better so!"

Then the nightingale flew away. The attendants came in to see after their dead emperor, and there he stood, bidding them "good-morning!"

The Steadfast Tin Soldier

There were once five and twenty tin soldiers, all brothers, for they were the offspring of the same old tin spoon. Each man shouldered his gun, kept his eyes well to the front, and wore the smartest red and blue uniform imaginable. The first thing they heard in their new world, when the lid was taken off the box, was a little boy clapping his hands and crying, "Soldiers, soldiers!" It was his birthday and they had just been given to him; so he lost no time in setting them up on the table. All the soldiers were exactly alike with one exception, and he differed from the rest in having only one leg. For he was made last, and there was not quite enough tin left to finish him. However, he stood just as well on his one leg as the others on two, in fact he is the very one who is to become famous. On the table where they were being set up, were many other toys; but the chief thing which caught the eye was a delightful paper castle. You could see through the tiny windows, right into the rooms. Outside there were some little trees surrounding a small mirror, representing a lake, whose surface reflected the waxen swans which were swimming about on it. It was altogether charming, but the prettiest thing of all was a little maiden standing at the open door of the castle. She, too, was cut out of paper, but she wore a dress of the lightest gauze, with a dainty little blue ribbon over her shoulders, by way of a scarf, set off by a brilliant spangle as big as her whole face. The little maid was stretching out both arms, for she was a dancer, and in the dance one of her legs was raised so high into the air that the tin soldier could see absolutely nothing of it, and supposed that she, like himself, had but one leg.

"That would be the very wife for me!" he thought; "but she is much too grand; she lives in a palace, while I only have a box, and then there are five and twenty of us to share it. No, that would be no place for her! but I must try to make her acquaintance!" Then he lay down full length behind a snuff box, which stood on the table. From that point he could have a good look at the little lady, who continued to stand on one leg without losing her balance.

Late in the evening the other soldiers were put into their box, and the people of the house went to bed. Now was the time for the toys to play; they amused themselves with paying visits, fighting battles, and giving balls. The tin soldiers rustled about in their box, for they wanted to join the games, but they could not get the lid off. The nut-crackers turned somersaults, and the pencil scribbled nonsense on the slate. There was such a noise that the canary woke up and joined in, but his remarks were in verse. The only two who did not move were the tin soldier and the little dancer. She stood as stiff as ever on tip-toe, with her arms spread out: he was equally firm on his one leg, and he did not take his eyes off her for a moment.

Then the clock struck twelve, when pop! up flew the lid of the snuff box, but there was no snuff in it, no! There was a little black goblin, a sort of Jack-in-the box.

"Tin soldier!" said the goblin, "have the goodness to keep your eyes to yourself."

But the tin soldier feigned not to hear.

"Ah! you just wait till tomorrow," said the goblin.

In the morning when the children got up they put the tin soldier on the window frame, and, whether it was caused by the goblin or by a puff of wind, I do not know, but all at once the window burst open, and the soldier fell head foremost from the third storey.

It was a terrific descent, and he landed at last, with his leg in the air, and rested on his cap, with his bayonet fixed between two paving stones. The maid-servant and the little boy ran down at once to look for him; but although they almost trod on him, they could not see him. Had the soldier only called out, "here I am," they would easily have found him, but he did not think it proper to shout when he was in uniform.

Presently it began to rain, and the drops fell faster and faster, till there was a regular torrent. When it was over two street boys came along.

"Look out!" said one; "there is a tin soldier! He shall go for a sail."

So they made a boat out of a newspaper and put the soldier into the middle of it, and he sailed away down the gutter; both boys ran alongside clapping their hands. Good heavens! what waves there were in the gutter, and what a current, but then it certainly had rained cats and dogs. The paper boat danced up and down, and now and then whirled round and round. A shudder ran through the tin soldier, but he remained undaunted, and did not move a muscle, only looked straight before him with his gun shouldered. All at once the boat drifted under a long wooden tunnel, and it became as dark as it was in his box.

"Where on earth am I going to now!" thought he. "Well,

well, it is all the fault of that goblin! Oh, if only the little maiden were with me in the boat it might be twice as dark for all I should care!"

At this moment a big water rat, who lived in the tunnel, came up.

"Have you a pass?" asked the rat. "Hand up your pass!"

The tin soldier did not speak, but clung still tighter to his gun. The boat rushed on, the rat close behind. Phew, how he gnashed his teeth and shouted to the bits of stick and straw,—

"Stop him, stop him, he hasn't paid his toll; he hasn't shown his pass!"

But the current grew stronger and stronger, the tin soldier could already see daylight before him at the end of the tunnel; but he also heard a roaring sound, fit to strike terror to the bravest heart. Just imagine! Where the tunnel ended the stream rushed straight into the big canal. That would be just as dangerous for him as it would be for us to shoot a great rapid. He was so near the end now that it was impossible to stop. The boat dashed out; the poor tin soldier held himself as stiff as he could; no one should say of him that he even winced.

The boat swirled round three or four times, and filled with water to the edge; it must sink. The tin soldier stood up to his neck in water, and the boat sank deeper and deeper. The paper became limper and limper, and at last the water went over his head—then he thought of the pretty little dancer, whom he was never to see again, and this refrain rang in his ears,—

> "Onward! Onward! Soldier!
> For death thou canst not shun."

At last the paper gave way entirely and the soldier fell through—but at the same moment he was swallowed by a big fish.

Oh! how dark it was inside the fish, it was worse than being in the tunnel even; and then it was so narrow! But the tin soldier was as dauntless as ever, and lay full length, shouldering his gun.

The fish rushed about and made the most frantic movements. At last it became quite quiet, and after a time, a flash like lightning pierced it. The soldier was once more in the broad daylight, and some one called out loudly, "a tin soldier!" The fish had been caught, taken to market, sold, and brought into the kitchen, where the cook cut it open with a large knife. She took the soldier up by the waist, with two fingers, and carried him into the parlour, where everyone wanted to see the wonderful man, who had travelled about in the stomach of a fish; but the tin soldier was not at all proud. They set him up on the table, and, wonder of wonders! he found himself in the very same room that he had been in before. He saw the very same children, and the toys were still standing on the table, as well as the beautiful castle with the pretty little dancer.

She still stood on one leg, and held the other up in the air. You see she also was unbending. The soldier was so much moved that he was ready to shed tears of tin, but that would not have been fitting. He looked at her, and she looked at him, but they said never a word. At this moment one of the little boys took up the tin soldier, and without rhyme or reason, threw him into the fire. No doubt the little goblin in the snuff box was to blame for that. The tin soldier stood there, lighted up by the flame, and in the most horrible heat;

but whether it was the heat of the real fire, or the warmth of his feelings, he did not know. He had lost all his gay colour; it might have been from his perilous journey, or it might have been from grief, who can tell?

He looked at the little maiden, and she looked at him; and he felt that he was melting away, but he still managed to keep himself erect, shouldering his gun bravely.

A door was suddenly opened, the draught caught the little dancer and she fluttered like a sylph, straight into the fire, to the soldier, blazed up and was gone!

By this time the soldier was reduced to a mere lump, and when the maid took away the ashes next morning she found him, in the shape of a small tin heart. All that was left of the dancer was her spangle, and that was burnt as black as a coal.

Thumbelisa

There was once a woman who had the greatest longing for
a little tiny child, but she had no idea where to get one; so she
went to an old witch and said to her, "I do so long to have a
little child, will you tell me where I can get one?"

"Oh, we shall be able to manage that," said the witch.
"Here is a barleycorn for you; it is not at all the same kind
as that which grows in the peasant's field, or with which
chickens are fed; plant it in a flower-pot and you will see what
will appear."

"Thank you, oh, thank you!" said the woman, and she
gave the witch twelve pennies, then went home and planted the
barley corn, and a large, handsome flower sprang up at once;
it looked exactly like a tulip, but the petals were tightly shut
up, just as if they were still in bud. "That is a lovely flower,"
said the woman, and she kissed the pretty red and yellow
petals; as she kissed it the flower burst open with a loud snap.
It was a real tulip, you could see that; but right in the middle
of the flower on the green stool sat a little tiny girl, most lovely
and delicate; she was not more than an inch in height, so she
was called Thumbelisa.

Her cradle was a smartly varnished walnut shell, with the
blue petals of violets for a mattress and a rose-leaf to cover
her; she slept in it at night, but during the day she played about
on the table where the woman had placed a plate, surrounded
by a wreath of flowers on the outer edge with their stalks in

water. A large tulip petal floated on the water, and on this little Thumbelisa sat and sailed about from one side of the plate to the other; she had two white horsehairs for oars. It was a pretty sight. She could sing, too, with such delicacy and charm as was never heard before.

One night as she lay in her pretty bed, a great ugly toad hopped in at the window, for there was a broken pane. Ugh! how hideous that great wet toad was; it hopped right down on to the table where Thumbelisa lay fast asleep, under the red rose-leaf.

"Here is a lovely wife for my son," said the toad, and then she took up the walnut shell where Thumbelisa slept and hopped away with it through the window, down into the garden. A great broad stream ran through it, but just at the edge it was swampy and muddy, and it was here that the toad lived with her son. Ugh! how ugly and hideous he was too, exactly like his mother. "Koax, koax, brekke-ke-kex, that was all he had to say when he saw the lovely little girl in the walnut shell.

"Do not talk so loud or you will wake her," said the old toad; "she might escape us yet, for she is as light as thistle-down! We will put her on one of the broad water-lily leaves out in the stream; it will be just like an island to her, she is so small and light. She won't be able to run away from there while we get the state-room ready down under the mud, which you are to inhabit."

A great many water lilies grew in the stream, their broad green leaves looked as if they were floating on the surface of the water. The leaf which was furthest from the shore was also the biggest, and to this one the old toad swam out with the walnut shell in which little Thumbelisa lay.

The poor, tiny little creature woke up quite early in the morning, and when she saw where she was she began to cry most bitterly, for there was water on every side of the big green leaf, and she could not reach the land at any point.

The old toad sat in the mud decking out her abode with grasses and the buds of the yellow water lilies, so as to have it very nice for the new daughter-in-law, and then she swam out with her ugly son to the leaf where Thumbelisa stood; they wanted to fetch her pretty bed to place it in the bridal chamber before they took her there. The old toad made a deep curtsey in the water before her, and said, "Here is my son, who is to be your husband, and you are to live together most comfortably down in the mud."

"Koax, koax, brekke-ke-kex," that was all the son could say.

Then they took the pretty little bed and swam away with it, but Thumbelisa sat quite alone on the green leaf and cried because she did not want to live with the ugly toad, or have her horrid son for a husband. The little fish which swam about in the water, had no doubt seen the toad and heard what she said, so they stuck their heads up, wishing, I suppose, to see the little girl. As soon as they saw her, they were delighted with her, and were quite grieved to think that she was to go down to live with the ugly toad. No, that should never happen. They flocked together down in the water round about the green stem which held the leaf she stood upon, and gnawed at it with their teeth till it floated away down the stream carrying Thumbelisa away where the toad could not follow her.

Thumbelisa sailed past place after place, and the little birds in the bushes saw her and sang, "what a lovely little maid."

The leaf with her on it floated further and further away and in this manner reached foreign lands.

A pretty little white butterfly fluttered round and round her for some time and at last settled on the leaf, for it had taken quite a fancy to Thumbelisa: she was so happy now, because the toad could not reach her and she was sailing through such lovely scenes; the sun shone on the water and it looked like liquid gold. Then she took her sash and tied one end round the butterfly, and the other she made fast to the leaf which went gliding on quicker and quicker, and she with it for she was standing on the leaf.

At this moment a big cockchafer came flying along, he caught sight of her and in an instant he fixed his claw round her slender waist and flew off with her, up into a tree, but the green leaf floated down the stream and the butterfly with it, for he was tied to it and could not get loose.

Heavens! how frightened poor little Thumbelisa was when the cockchafer carried her up into the tree, but she was most of all grieved about the pretty white butterfly which she had fastened to the leaf; if he could not succeed in getting loose he would be starved to death.

But the cockchafer cared nothing for that. He settled with her on the largest leaf on the tree, and fed her with honey from the flowers, and he said that she was lovely although she was not a bit like a chafer. Presently all the other chafers which lived in the tree came to visit them; they looked at Thumbelisa and the young lady chafers twitched their feelers and said, "she has also got two legs, what a good effect it has." "She has no feelers," said another. "She is so slender in the waist, fie, she looks like a human being." "How ugly she is," said all the mother chafers, and yet little Thumbelisa was so pretty. That was certainly also the opinion of the cockchafer who had captured her, but when all the others said she was ugly, he at last began to believe it too, and would not have anything more to do with her, she might go wherever she liked! They flew down from the tree with her and placed her on a daisy, where she cried because she was so ugly that the chafers would have nothing to do with her; and after all, she was more beautiful than anything you could imagine, as delicate and transparent as the finest rose-leaf.

Poor little Thumbelisa lived all the summer quite alone in the wood. She plaited a bed of grass for herself and hung it up under a big dock-leaf which sheltered her from the rain; she sucked the honey from the flowers for her food, and her drink was the dew which lay on the leaves in the morning. In this way the summer and autumn passed, but then came the winter. All the birds which used to sing so sweetly to her flew away, the great dock-leaf under which she had lived shrivelled up, leaving nothing but a dead yellow stalk, and she shivered with the cold, for her clothes were worn out; she was such a tiny creature, poor little Thumbelisa, she certainly must be frozen to death. It began to snow and every snow-flake which fell upon her was like a whole shovelful upon one of us, for we are big and she was only one inch in height. Then she wrapped herself up in a withered leaf, but that did not warm her much, she trembled with the cold.

Close to the wood in which she had been living lay a large cornfield, but the corn had long ago been carried away and nothing remained but the bare, dry, stubble which stood up out of the frozen ground. The stubble was quite a forest for her to walk about in: oh, how she shook with the cold. Then she came to the door of a field-mouse's home. It was a little hole down under the stubble. The field-mouse lived so cosily and warm there, her whole room was full of corn, and she had a beautiful kitchen and larder besides. Poor Thumbelisa stood just inside the door like any other poor beggar child and begged for a little piece of barley corn, for she had had nothing to eat for two whole days.

"You poor little thing," said the field-mouse, for she was at bottom a good old field-mouse. "Come into my warm room and dine with me." Then, as she took a fancy to Thumbelisa, she said, "you may with pleasure stay with me for the winter, but you must keep my room clean and tidy and tell me stories, for I am very fond of them," and Thumbelisa did what the good old field-mouse desired and was on the whole very comfortable.

"Now we shall soon have a visitor," said the field-mouse; "my neighbour generally comes to see me every week-day. He is even better housed than I am; his rooms are very large and he wears a most beautiful black velvet coat; if only you could get him for a husband you would indeed be well settled, but he can't see. You must tell him all the most beautiful stories you know."

But Thumbelisa did not like this, and she would have nothing to say to the neighbour, for he was a mole. He came and paid a visit in his black velvet coat. He was very rich and wise, said the field-mouse, and his home was twenty times as large as hers; and he had much learning, but he did not like the sun or the beautiful flowers, in fact he spoke slightingly of them, for he had never seen them. Thumbelisa had to sing to him and she sang both "Fly away cockchafer" and "A monk, he wandered through the meadow," then the mole fell in love with her because of her sweet voice, but he did not say anything, for he was of a discreet turn of mind.

He had just made a long tunnel through the ground from his house to theirs, and he gave the field-mouse and Thumbelisa leave to walk in it whenever they liked. He told them not to be afraid of the dead bird which was lying in the passage. It was a whole bird with feathers and beak which had probably died quite recently at the beginning of the winter, and was now entombed just where he had made his tunnel.

The mole took a piece of tinder-wood in his mouth, for that shines like fire in the dark, and walked in front of them to light them in the long dark passage; when they came to the place where the dead bird lay, the mole thrust his broad nose up to the roof and pushed the earth up so as to make a big hole through which the daylight shone. In the middle of the floor lay a dead swallow, with its pretty wings closely pressed to its sides, and the legs and head drawn in under the feathers; no doubt the poor bird had died of cold. Thumbelisa was so sorry for it; she loved all the little birds, for they had twittered and sung so sweetly to her during the whole summer; but the mole kicked it with his short legs and said, "Now it will pipe no more! it must be a miserable fate to be born a little bird! Thank heaven! no child of mine can be a bird; a bird like that has nothing but its twitter and dies of hunger in the winter."

"Yes, as a sensible man, you may well say that," said the field-mouse. "What *has* a bird for all its twittering when the cold weather comes? it has to hunger and freeze, but then it must cut a dash."

Thumbelisa did not say anything, but when the others turned their backs to the bird, she stooped down and stroked aside the feathers which lay over its head, and kissed its closed eyes. "Perhaps it was this very bird which sang so sweetly to me in the summer," she thought; "what pleasure it gave me, the dear pretty bird."

The mole now closed up the hole which let in the daylight and conducted the ladies to their home. Thumbelisa could not sleep at all in the night, so she got up out of her bed and plaited a large handsome mat of hay and then she carried it down and spread it all over the dead bird, and laid some soft cotton wool which she had found in the field-mouse's room close round its sides, so that it might have a warm bed on the cold ground.

"Good-bye you sweet little bird," said she, "good-bye, and thank you for your sweet song through the summer, when all the trees were green and the sun shone warmly upon us." Then she laid her head close up to the bird's breast, but was quite startled at a sound, as if something was thumping inside it. It was the bird's heart. It was not dead but lay in a swoon, and now that it had been warmed it began to revive.

In the autumn all the swallows fly away to warm countries, but if one happens to be belated, it feels the cold so much that it falls down like a dead thing, and remains lying where it falls till the snow covers it up. Thumbelisa quite shook with fright, for the bird was very, very big beside her who was only one inch high, but she gathered up her courage, packed the wool closer round the poor bird, and fetched a leaf of mint which he had herself for a coverlet and laid it over the bird's head. The next night she stole down again to it and found it alive, but so feeble that it could only just open its eyes for a moment to look at Thumbelisa who stood with a bit of tinder-wood in her hand, for she had no other lantern. "Many, many thanks, you sweet child," said the sick swallow to her; "you have warmed me beautifully. I shall soon have strength to fly out into the warm sun again."

"Oh!" said she, "it is so cold outside, it snows and freezes, stay in your warm bed, I will tend you." Then she brought water to the swallow in a leaf, and when it had drunk some, it told her how it had torn its wing on a blackthorn bush, and therefore could not fly as fast as the other swallows which were taking flight then for the distant warm lands. At last it fell down on the ground, but after that it remembered nothing, and did not in the least know how it had got into the tunnel.

It stayed there all the winter, and Thumbelisa was good to it and grew very fond of it. She did not tell either the mole or the field-mouse anything about it, for they did not like the poor unfortunate swallow.

As soon as the spring came and the warmth of the sun penetrated the ground, the swallow said good-bye to Thumbelisa, who opened the hole which the mole had made above. The sun streamed in deliciously upon them, and the swallow asked if she would not go with him, she could sit upon his back and they would fly far away into the green wood. But Thumbelisa knew that it would grieve the old field mouse if she left her like that.

"No, I can't," said Thumbelisa.

"Good-bye, good-bye, then, you kind pretty girl," said the swallow, and flew out into the sunshine. Thumbelisa looked after him and her eyes filled with tears, for she was very fond of the poor swallow.

"Tweet, tweet," sang the bird, and flew into the green wood. Thumbelisa was very sad. She was not allowed to go out into the warm sunshine at all; the corn which was sown in the field near the field-mouse's house grew quite long, it was a thick forest for the poor little girl who was only an inch high.

"You must work at your trousseau this summer," said the mouse to her, for their neighbour the tiresome mole in his black velvet coat had asked her to marry him. "You shall have both woollen and linen, you shall have wherewith to clothe and cover yourself when you become the mole's wife." Thumbelisa had to turn the distaff and the field-mouse hired four spiders to spin and weave day and night. The mole paid a visit every evening, and he was always saying that when the summer came to an end, the sun would not shine nearly so warmly, now it burnt the ground as hard as a stone. Yes, when the summer was over he would celebrate his marriage; but Thumbelisa was not at all pleased, for she did not care a bit for the tiresome mole. Every morning at sunrise and every evening at sunset she used to steal out to the door, and when the wind blew aside the tops of the cornstalks so that she could see the blue sky, she thought how bright and lovely it was out there, and wished so much to see the dear swallow again: but it never came back; no doubt it was a long way off, flying about in the beautiful green woods.

When the autumn came all Thumbelisa's outfit was ready.

"In four weeks you must be married," said the field-mouse to her. But Thumbelisa cried and said that she would not have the tiresome mole for a husband.

"Fiddle-dee-dee," said the field-mouse; "don't be obstinate or I shall bite you with my white tooth. You are going to have a splendid husband; the queen herself hasn't the equal of his black velvet coat; both his kitchen and his cellar are full. You should thank heaven for such a husband!"

So they were to be married; the mole had come to fetch Thumbelisa; she was to live deep down under the ground with him, and never to go out into the warm sunshine, for he could not bear it. The poor child was very sad at the thought of bidding good-bye to the beautiful sun; while she had been with the field-mouse she had at least been allowed to look at it from the door.

"Good-bye, you bright sun," she said as she stretched out her arms towards it and went a little way outside the field-mouse's house, for now the harvest was over and only the stubble remained. "Good-bye, good-bye!" she said, and threw her tiny arms round a little red flower growing there. "Give my love to the dear swallow if you happen to see him."

"Tweet, tweet," she heard at this moment above her head. She looked up; it was the swallow just passing. As soon as it saw Thumbelisa it was delighted; she told it how unwilling she was to have the ugly mole for a husband, and that she was to live deep down underground where the sun never shone. She could not help crying about it.

"The cold winter is coming," said the swallow, "and I am going to fly away to warm countries. Will you go with me? You can sit upon my back! Tie yourself on with your sash, then we will fly away from the ugly mole and his dark cavern, far away over the mountains to those warm countries where the sun shines with greater splendour than here, where it is always summer and there are heaps of flowers. Do fly with me, you sweet little Thumbelisa, who saved my life when I lay frozen in the dark earthy passage."

"Yes, I will go with you," said Thumbelisa, seating herself on the bird's back with her feet on its out-spread wing. She tied her band tightly to one of the strongest feathers, and then the swallow flew away, high up in the air above forest and lakes, high up above the biggest mountains where the snow never melts; and Thumbelisa shivered in the cold air, but then she crept under the bird's warm feathers, and only stuck out her little head to look at the beautiful sights beneath her.

Then at last they reached the warm countries. The sun shone with a warmer glow than here; the sky was twice as high, and the most beautiful green and blue grapes grew in clusters on the banks and hedgerows. Oranges and lemons hung in the woods which were fragrant with myrtles and sweet herbs, and beautiful children ran about the roads playing with the large gorgeously-coloured butterflies. But the swallow flew on and on, and the country grew more and more beautiful. Under magnificent green trees on the shores of the blue sea stood a dazzling white marble palace of ancient date; vines wreathed themselves round the stately pillars. At the head of these there were countless nests, and the swallow who carried Thumbelisa lived in one of them.

"Here is my house," said the swallow; "but if you will choose one of the gorgeous flowers growing down there, I will place you in it, and you will live as happily as you can wish."

"That would be delightful," she said, and clapped her little hands.

A great white marble column had fallen to the ground and lay there broken in three pieces, but between these the most lovely white flowers grew. The swallow flew down with Thumbelisa and put her upon one of the broad leaves; what was her astonishment to find a little man in the middle of the flower, as bright and transparent as if he had been made of glass. He had a lovely golden crown upon his head and the most beautiful bright wings upon his shoulders; he was no bigger than Thumbelisa. He was the angel of the flowers. There was a similar little man or woman in every flower, but he was the king of them all.

"Heavens, how beautiful he is," whispered Thumbelisa to the swallow. The little prince was quite frightened by the swallow, for it was a perfect giant of a bird to him, he who was so small and delicate, but when he saw Thumbelisa he was delighted; she was the very prettiest girl he had ever seen. He therefore took the golden crown off his own head and placed it on hers, and asked her name, and if she would be his wife, and then she would be queen of the flowers! Yes, he was certainly a very different kind of husband from the toad's son, or the mole with his black velvet coat. So she accepted the beautiful prince, and out of every flower stepped a little lady or a gentleman so lovely that it was a pleasure to look at them. Each one brought a gift to Thumbelisa, but the best of all was a pair of pretty wings from a large white fly; they were fastened on to her back, and then she too could fly from flower to flower. All was then delight and happiness, but the swallow sat alone in his nest and sang to them as well as he could, for his heart was heavy, he was so fond of Thumbelisa himself, and would have wished never to part from her.

"You shall not be called Thumbelisa," said the angel of the flower to her; "that is such an ugly name, and you are so pretty. We will call you May."

"Good-bye, good-bye," said the swallow, and flew away again from the warm countries, far away back to Denmark; there he had a little nest above the window where the man lived who wrote this story, and he sang his "tweet, tweet" to the man, and so we have the whole story.

The Storks

A stork had built his nest on the roof of the last house in a little town. The mother-stork was sitting on the nest with her little ones, who stuck out their little black beaks, which had not turned red yet. The father-stork stood a little way off on the ridge of the roof, erect and stiff, with one leg drawn up under him, so as at least to be at some trouble while standing sentry. One might have thought he was carved out of wood, he stood so still!

"It will look so grand for my wife to have a sentry on guard by the nest!" he thought. "People won't know that I am her husband. I daresay they think I have orders to stand there—it looks smart!" and so he remained standing on one leg.

A party of children were playing in the street, and when they saw the stork, one of the boldest boys, followed by the others, sang the old song about the storks, but he sang it just as it came into his head,—

> "Oh! father stork, father stork, fly to your nest,
> Three featherless fledglings await your return.
> The first of your chicks shall be stuck through the breast
> The second shall hang and the third shall burn."

"Hark! what are the boys singing?" said the little storks; "they say we are to be hanged and burnt!"

"Don't bother your heads about them!" said the mother-stork; "don't listen to them and then it won't do you any harm."

But the boys went on singing and pointing their fingers at the storks; only one boy, whose name was Peter, said that it was a shame to make fun of the creatures and he would take no part in it.

The mother bird comforted her little ones saying, "Do not trouble yourselves about it, look at your father how quietly he stands, and on one leg too!"

"But we are so frightened," said the young ones, burying their heads in the nest.

The next day when the children came back to play and they saw the storks they began their old song,—

> "The first of your chicks shall be stuck through the breast
> The second shall hang and the third shall burn."

"Are we to be hanged and burnt?" asked the little storks.

"No, certainly not!" said the mother; "you are to learn to fly, see if I don't drill you, then we will go into the fields and visit the frogs; they curtsey in the water to us and sing 'Koax, Koax,' and then we gobble them up; that's a treat if you like!"

"And what next?" asked the young ones.

"Oh, then all the storks in the country assemble for the autumn manoeuvres, and you will have to fly your best, for the one who cannot fly will be run through the body by the general's beak, so you must take good care to learn something when the drills begin."

"After all then we may be staked just as the boys said, and listen, they are singing it again now!"

"Listen to me and not to them," said the mother stork. "After the grand manoeuvres we shall fly away to the warm countries, ever such a way off, over the woods and mountains. We go to Egypt where they have three-cornered houses, the

points of which reach above the clouds; they are called Pyramids, and they are older than any stork can imagine. Then there is a river which overflows its banks and all the land round turns to mud. You walk about in mud devouring frogs."

"Oh!" said all the young ones.

"Yes, it is splendid, you do nothing but eat all day; while we are so well off there, there is not a leaf on the trees in this country, and it is so cold that the clouds freeze all to pieces and fall down in little bits."

She meant snow, but did not know how to describe it any better.

"Do the naughty boys freeze to pieces?" asked the young storks.

"No, they don't freeze to pieces, but they come very near to it and have to sit moping in dark rooms; you, on the other hand, fly about in strange countries, in the warm sunshine among flowers."

Some time passed and the little ones were big enough to stand up in the nest and look about them. The father stork flew backwards and forwards every day, with nice frogs and little snakes, and every kind of delicacy he could find. It was so funny to see the tricks he did to amuse them; he would turn his head right round on to his tail, and he would clatter with his beak, as if it was a rattle. And then he told them all the stories he heard in the swamps.

"Well, now you must learn to fly," said the mother stork one day; and all the young ones had to stand on the ridge of the roof. Oh, how they wobbled about trying to keep their balance with their wings, and how nearly they fell down.

"Now look at me," said the mother; "this is how you must

hold your heads! And move your legs so! one, two, one, two, this will all help you to get on in the world."

Then she flew a little way, and the young ones made a clumsy little hop, and down they came with a bump, for their bodies were too heavy.

"I don't want to fly," said one of the young ones, creeping down into the nest again. "I don't care about going to the warm countries."

"Do you want to freeze to death here when the winter comes? Shall the boys come and hang or burn or stake you? I will soon call them!"

"No, no," said the young one, hopping up on to the roof again, just like the others.

By the third day they could all fly fairly well; then they thought they could hover in the air, too, and they tried it, but flop!—they soon found they had to move their wings again.

Then the boys began their song again,—

"Oh! father stork, father stork, fly to your nest."

"Shall we fly down and pick their eyes out?" asked the young ones.

"No, leave them alone," said their mother; "only pay attention to me, that is much more important. One, two, three, now we fly to the right; one, two, three, now to the left, and round the chimney! that was good. That last stroke of the wings was so pretty and the flap so well done that I will allow you to go to the swamp with me to-morrow! Several nice storks go there with their children; now just let me see that mine are the nicest. Don't forget to carry your heads high; it looks well, and gives you an air of importance."

"But are we not to have our revenge on the naughty boys?" asked the young storks.

"Let them scream as much as they like; you will fly away with the clouds to the land of the pyramids, while they will perhaps be freezing. There won't be a green leaf or a sweet apple here then!"

"But we *will* have our revenge!" they whispered to each other, and then they began their drilling again.

Of all the boys in the street, not one was worse at making fun of the storks than he who first began the derisive song. He was a tiny little fellow, not more than six years old. It is true, the young storks thought he was at least a hundred, for he was so much bigger than their father and mother and they had no idea how old children and grown-up people could be. They reserved all their vengeance for the boy who first began to teaze them, and who never would leave off. The young storks were frightfully irritated by the teazing, and the older they grew the less they would stand it. At last their mother was obliged to promise that they should have their revenge, but not till the last day before they left.

"We shall first have to see how you behave at the manoeuvres! If you come to grief and the general has to run you through the breast with his beak, the boys will after all be right, at least in one way! Now let us see!"

"That you shall!" said the young ones, and didn't they take pains. They practised every day, till they could fly as lightly as any feather; it was quite a pleasure to watch them.

Then came the autumn; all the storks began to assemble, before they started on their flight to the warm countries, where they spend their winters.

Those were indeed manoeuvres! They had to fly over woods

and towns, to try their wings, because they had such a long journey before them. The young storks did everything so well that they got no end of frogs and snakes as prizes. They had the best characters, and then they could eat the frogs and snakes afterwards, which you may be sure they did.

"Now we shall have our revenge!" they said.

"Yes, certainly," said the mother stork. "My plan is this, and I think it is the right one! I know the pond where all the little human babies lie, till the storks fetch them, and give them to their parents. The pretty little creatures lie there asleep, dreaming sweet dreams, sweeter than any they ever dream afterwards. Every parent wishes for such a little baby, and every child wants a baby brother or sister. Now we fly to the pond and fetch a little brother or sister for each of those children who did not join in singing that horrid song, or in making fun of the storks. But those who sang it shall not have one."

"But what about that bad wicked boy who first began the song!" shrieked the young storks; "what is to be done to him?"

"In the pond there is a little dead baby, it has dreamed itself to death, we will take it to him, and then he will cry, because we have brought him a little dead brother. But you have surely not forgotten the good boy, who said, 'It is a shame to make fun of the creatures!' We will take both a brother and a sister to him, and because his name is Peter, you shall all be called Peter too."

It happened just as she said, and all the storks are called Peter to this day.

Great Claus and Little Claus

In a village there once lived two men of the self-same name. They were both called Claus, but one of them had four horses, and the other had only one; so to distinguish them people called the owner of the four horses "Great Claus," and he who had only one "Little Claus."

Now I shall tell you what happened to them, for this is a true story.

Throughout the week Little Claus was obliged to plough for Great Claus, and to lend him his one horse; but once a week, on Sunday. Great Claus lent him all his four horses.

"Hurrah!" How Little Claus would smack his whip over all five, for they were as good as his own on that one day.

The sun shone brightly and the church bells rang merrily as the people passed by, dressed in their best, with their prayer-books under their arms. They were going to hear the parson preach. They looked at Little Claus ploughing with his five horses, and he was so proud that he smacked his whip and said, "Gee-up, my five horses."

"You mustn't say that," said Great Claus, "for only one of them is yours."

But Little Claus soon forgot what he ought not to say, and when anyone passed, he would call out, "Gee-up, my five horses."

"I must really beg you not to say that again," said Great Claus, "for if you do, I shall hit your horse on the head, so that he will drop down dead on the spot, and there will be an end of him."

"I promise you I will not say it again," said the other; but as soon as anybody came by nodding to him, and wishing him "Good-day," he was so pleased, and thought how grand it was to have five horses ploughing in his field, that he cried out again, "Gee-up, all my horses!"

"I'll gee-up your horses for you," said Great Claus, and seizing the tethering mallet he struck Little Claus' one horse on the head, and it fell down dead.

"Oh, now I have no horse at all," said Little Claus, weeping. But after a while he flayed the dead horse, and hung up the skin in the wind to dry.

Then he put the dried skin into a bag, and hanging it over his shoulder went off to the next town to sell it. But he had a long way to go, and had to pass through a dark and gloomy forest.

Presently a storm arose, and he lost his way; and before he discovered the right path evening was drawing on, and it was still a long way to the town, and too far to return home before nightfall.

Near the road stood a large farmhouse. The shutters outside the windows were closed, but lights shone through the crevices and at the top. "They might let me stay here for the night," thought Little Claus, so he went up to the door and knocked. The farmer's wife opened the door, but when she heard what he wanted, she told him to go away; her husband was not at home, and she could not let any strangers in.

"Then I shall have to lie out here," said Little Claus to himself as the farmer's wife shut the door in his face.

Close to the farmhouse stood a large haystack, and between

it and the house there was a small shed with a thatched roof. "I can lie up there," said little Claus, as he saw the roof; "it will make a famous bed, but I hope the stork won't fly down and bite my legs." A live stork was standing up there who had his nest on the roof.

So Little Claus climbed on to the roof of the shed, and as he turned about to make himself comfortable he discovered that the wooden shutters did not reach to the top of the windows, so that he could see into the room, in which a large table was laid out, with wine, roast meat, and a splendid fish.

The farmer's wife and the sexton were sitting at table together, nobody else was there. She was filling his glass and helping him plentifully to fish, which appeared to be his favourite dish.

"If only I could have some too," thought Little Claus, and then as he stretched out his neck towards the window he spied a beautiful, large cake—indeed, they had a glorious feast before them.

At that moment he heard someone riding down the road towards the farm. It was the farmer coming home.

He was a good man, but he had one very strange prejudice—he could not bear the sight of a sexton. If he happened to see one he would get into a terrible rage. In consequence of this dislike, the sexton had gone to visit the farmer's wife during her husband's absence from home, and the good woman had put before him the best of everything she had in the house to eat.

When they heard the farmer they were dreadfully frightened, and the woman made the sexton creep into a large chest which stood in a corner. He went at once, for he was well aware of the poor man's aversion to the sight of a sexton. The woman then quickly hid all the nice things and the wine in the oven, because if her husband had seen it he would have asked why it was provided.

"Oh, dear!" sighed Little Claus, on the roof, when he saw the food disappearing.

"Is there anyone up there?" asked the farmer, peering up at Little Claus. "What are you doing up there? You had better come into the house."

Then Little Claus told him how he had lost his way, and asked if he might have shelter for the night.

"Certainly," said the farmer; "but the first thing is to have something to eat."

The woman received them both very kindly, laid the table, and gave them a large bowl of porridge. The farmer was hungry and ate it with a good appetite; but Little Claus could not help thinking of the good roast meat, the fish, and the cake, which he knew were hidden in the oven.

He had put his sack with the hide in it under the table by his feet, for, as we remember, he was on his way to the town to sell it. He did not fancy the porridge, so he trod on the sack and made the dried hide squeak quite loudly.

"Hush!" said Little Claus to his sack, at the same time treading on it again, so that it squeaked louder than ever.

"What on earth have you go in your sack?" asked the farmer again.

"Oh, it's a Goblin," said Little Claus; "he says we needn't eat the porridge, for he has charmed the oven full of roast meat and fish and cake."

"What do you say!" said the farmer, opening the oven door with all speed, and seeing the nice things the woman had hidden, but which her husband thought the Goblin had produced for their special benefit. The woman dared not say anything, but put the food before them, and then they both made a hearty meal of the fish, the meat, and the cake. Then Little Claus trod on the skin and made it squeak again.

"What does he say now?" asked the farmer.

"He says," answered Little Claus, "that he has also charmed three bottles of wine into the oven for us."

So the woman had to bring out the wine too, and the farmer drank it and became very merry. Wouldn't he like to have a Goblin, like the one in Little Claus' sack, for himself?

"Can he charm out the Devil?" asked the farmer. "I shouldn't mind seeing him, now that I am in such a merry mood."

"Oh yes!" said Little Claus; "my Goblin can do everything that we ask him. Can't you?" he asked, trampling up the sack till it squeaked louder than ever. "Do you hear what I say? But the Devil is so ugly, you'd better not see him."

"Oh! I'm not a bit frightened. Whatever does he look like?"

"Well, he will show himself in the image of a sexton."

"Oh, dear!" said the farmer; "that's bad! I must tell you that I can't bear to see a sexton! However, it doesn't matter; I shall know it's only the Devil, and then I shan't mind so much! Now, my courage is up! But he mustn't come too close."

"I'll ask my Goblin about it," said Little Claus, treading on the bag and putting his ear close to it.

"What does he say?"

"He says you can go along and open the chest in the corner, and there you'll see the Devil moping in the dark; but hold the lid tight so that he doesn't get out."

"Will you help me to hold it!" asked the farmer, going along to the chest where the woman had hidden the real sexton, who was shivering with fright.

The farmer lifted up the lid a wee little bit and peeped in. "Ha!" he shrieked, and sprang back. "Yes, I saw him, and he looked just exactly like our sexton! It was a horrible sight."

They had to have a drink after this, and there they sat drinking till far into the night.

"You must sell me that Goblin," said the farmer. "You may ask what you like! I'll give you a bushel of money for him."

"No, I can't do that," said Little Claus; "you must remember how useful my Goblin is to me."

"Oh, but I should so like to have him," said the farmer, and he went on begging for him.

"Well," said Little Claus at last, "as you have been so kind to me I shall have to give him up. "You shall have my Goblin for a bushel of money, but I must have it full to the brim!"

"You shall have it," said the farmer; "but you must take that chest away with you; I won't have it in the house for another hour; you never know whether he's there or not."

So Little Claus gave his sack with the dried hide in it to the farmer, and received in return a bushel of money for it and the measure was full to the brim. The farmer also gave him a large wheelbarrow to take the money and the chest away in.

"Good-bye!" said Little Claus, and off he went with his money and the big chest with the sexton in it.

There was a wide and deep river on the other side of the wood, the stream was so strong that it was almost impossible to swim against it. A large new bridge had been built across it, and when they got into the very middle of it, Little Claus said quite loud, so that the sexton could hear him—

"What am I to do with this stupid old chest? it might be full of paving stones, it's so heavy! I am quite tired of wheeling it along; I'll just throw it into the river; if it floats down the river to my house, well and good, and if it doesn't, I shan't care."

Then he took hold of the chest and raised it up a bit, as if he was about to throw it into the river.

"No, no! let it be!" shouted the sexton; "let me get out!"

"Hullo!" said Little Claus, pretending to be frightened. "Why, he's still inside it, then I must have it into the river to drown him."

"Oh no, oh no!" shouted the sexton. "I'll give you a bushel full of money if you'll let me out!"

"Oh, that's another matter," said Little Claus, opening the chest. The sexton crept out at once and pushed the empty chest into the water, and then went home and gave Little Claus a whole bushel full of money: he had already had one from the farmer, you know, so now his wheelbarrow was quite full of money.

"I got a pretty fair price for that horse I must admit!" said he to himself when he got home to his own room and turned the money out of the wheelbarrow into a heap on the floor. "What a rage Great Claus will be in when he discovers how rich I am become through my one horse, but I won't tell him straight out about it." So he sent a boy to Great Claus to borrow a bushel measure.

"What does he want that for!" thought Great Claus, and he rubbed some tallow on the bottom, so that a little of whatever was to be measured might stick to it. So it did, for when the measure came back three new silver threepenny bits were sticking to it.

"What's this?" said Great Claus, and he ran straight along to Little Claus. "Where on earth did you get all that money?"

"Oh, that was for my horse's hide which I sold last night."

"That was well paid indeed," said Great Claus, and he ran home, took an axe and hit all his four horses on the head. He then flayed them and went off to the town with the hides.

"Skins, skins, who will buy skins?" he shouted up and down the streets.

All the shoemakers and tanners in the town came running up and asked him how much he wanted for them.

"A bushel of money for each," said Great Claus.

"Are you mad?" they all said; "do you imagine we have money by the bushel?"

"Skins, skins, who will buy skins?" he shouted again, and the shoemakers took up their measures and the tanners their leather aprons, and beat Great Claus through the town.

"Skins, skins!" they mocked him. "Yes, we'll give you a raw hide. Out of the town with him!" they shouted, and Great Claus had to hurry off as fast as ever he could go. He had never had such a beating in his life.

"Little Claus shall pay for this!" he said when he got home. "I'll kill him for it."

Little Claus' old grandmother had just died in his house; she certainly had been very cross and unkind to him, but now that she was dead he felt quite sorry about it. He took the dead woman and put her into his warm bed, to see if he could bring her to life again. He meant her to stay there all night, and he would sit on a chair in the corner; he had slept like that before.

As he sat there in the night, the door opened, and in came Great Claus with his axe; he knew where Little Claus' bed stood, and he went straight up to it and hit the dead grandmother a blow on the forehead, thinking that it was Little Claus.

"Just see if you'll cheat me again after that!" he said, and then he went home again.

"What a bad, wicked man he is," said Little Claus; "he was going to kill me there. What a good thing that poor old granny was dead already, or else he would have killed her."

He now dressed his old grandmother in her best Sunday clothes, borrowed a horse of his neighbour, harnessed it to a cart, and set his grandmother on the back seat, so that she could not fall out when the cart moved. Then he started off through the wood. When the sun rose he was just outside a big inn, and Little Claus drew up his horse and went in to get something to eat. The landlord was a very, very rich man, and a very good man, but he was fiery-tempered, as if he were made of pepper and tobacco.

"Good morning!" said he to Little Claus; "you've got your best clothes on very early this morning!"

"Yes," said Little Claus; "I'm going to town with my old grandmother, she's sitting out there in the cart, I can't get her to come in. Won't you take her out a glass of mead? You'll have to shout at her, she's very hard of hearing."

"Yes, she shall have it!" said the innkeeper, and he poured out a large glass of mead which he took out to the dead grandmother in the cart.

"Here is a glass of mead your son has sent!" said the innkeeper, but the dead woman sat quite still and never said a word.

"Don't you hear?" shouted the innkeeper as loud as ever he could; "here is a glass of mead from your son!"

Again he shouted, and then again as loud as ever, but as she did not stir, he got angry and threw the glass of mead in her face, so that the mead ran all over her, and she fell backwards out of the cart, for she was only stuck up and not tied in.

"Now!" shouted Little Claus, as he rushed out of the inn and seized the landlord by the neck, "you have killed my grandmother! Just look, there's a great hole in her forehead!"

"Oh, what a misfortune!" exclaimed the innkeeper, clasping his hands; "that's the consequence of my fiery temper! Good Little Claus, I will give you a bushel of money, and bury your grandmother as if she had been my own, if you will only say nothing about it, or else they will chop my head off, and that is so nasty."

So Little Claus had a whole bushel of money, and the innkeeper buried the old grandmother just as if she had been his own.

When Little Claus got home again with all his money, he immediately sent over his boy to Great Claus to borrow his measure.

"What!" said Great Claus, "is he not dead? I shall have to go and see about it myself!" So he took the measure over to Little Claus himself.

"I say, wherever did you get all that money?" asked he, his eyes, round with amazement at what he saw.

"It was my grandmother you killed instead of me!" said Little Claus. "I have sold her and got a bushel of money for her!"

"That was good pay indeed!" said Great Claus, and he hurried home, took an axe and killed his old grandmother.

He then put her in a cart and drove off to the town where the apothecary lived, and asked if he would buy a dead body,

"Who is it, and where did the body come from?" asked the apothecary.

"It is my grandmother, and I have killed her for a bushel of money!" said Great Claus.

"Heaven preserve us!" said the apothecary. "You are talking like a madman; pray don't say such things, you might lose your head!"

And he pointed out to him what a horribly wicked thing he had done, and what a bad man he was who deserved punishment. Great Claus was so frightened that he rushed straight out of the shop, jumped into the cart, whipped up his horse and galloped home. The apothecary and everyone else thought he was mad, and so they let him drive off.

"You shall be paid for this!" said Great Claus, when he got out on the high road. "You shall pay for this, Little Claus!"

As soon as he got home, he took the biggest sack he could find, went over to Little Claus and said,—

"You have deceived me again! First I killed my horses, and then my old grandmother! It's all your fault, but you shan't have the chance of cheating me again!"

Then he took Little Claus by the waist and put him into the sack, put it on his back, and shouted to him—"I'm going to drown you now!"

It was a long way to go before he came to the river, and Little Claus was not so light to carry. The road passed close by the church in which the organ was playing, and the people were singing beautifully. Great Claus put down the sack with Little Claus in it close by the church door, and thought he would like to go and hear a psalm before he went any further. Little Claus could not get out of the bag, and all the people were in church, so Great Claus went in too.

"Oh dear, oh dear!" sighed Little Claus in the sack. He turned and twisted, but it was impossible to undo the cord. Just then an old cattle drover with white hair and a tall stick in his hand came along. He had a whole drove of cows and bulls before him; they ran against the sack Little Claus was in, and upset it.

"Oh dear!" sighed Little Claus; "I am so young to be going to the Kingdom of Heaven!"

"And I," said the cattle drover, "am so old and cannot get there yet!"

"Open the sack!" shouted Little Claus. "Get in in place of me, and you will get to heaven directly!"

"That will just suit me," said the cattle drover, undoing the sack for Little Claus, who immediately sprang out. "You must look after the cattle now," said the old man as he crept into the sack. Little Claus tied it up and walked off driving the cattle before him.

A little while after Great Claus came out of the church, he took up the sack again on his back, and certainly thought it had grown lighter, for the old cattle drover was not more than half the weight of Little Claus.

"How light he seems to have got; that must be because I have been to church and said my prayers!" Then he went on to the river, which was both wide and deep, and threw the sack with the old cattle drover in it into the water, shouting as he did so (for he thought it was Little Claus), "Now, you won't cheat me again!" Then he went homewards, but when he reached the crossroads he met Little Claus with his herd of cattle

"What's the meaning of this!" exclaimed Great Claus; "didn't I drown you?"

"Yes," said little Claus, "it's just about half an hour since you threw me into the river!"

"But where did you get all those splendid beasts?" asked Great Claus.

"They are sea-cattle," said Little Claus. "I will tell you the whole story, and indeed I thank you heartily for drowning me, I'm at the top of the tree now and a very rich man, I can tell you. I was so frightened when I was in the sack, the wind whistled in my ears when you threw me over the bridge into the cold water. I immediately sank to the bottom, but I was not hurt, for the grass is beautifully soft down there. The sack was opened at once by a beautiful maiden in snow-white clothes with a green wreath on her wet hair; she took my hand and said, 'Are you there, Little Claus? Here are some cattle for you, and a mile further up the road you will come upon another herd, which I will give you too!' Then I saw that the river was a great highway for the sea-folk. Down at the bottom of it they walked and drove about, from the sea right up to the end of the river. The flowers were lovely and the grass was so fresh; the fishes which swam about glided close to me just like birds in the air. How nice the people were, and what a lot of cattle strolling about in the ditches."

"But why did you come straight up here again then?" asked Great Claus. "I shouldn't have done that, if it was so fine down there."

"Oh," said Little Claus, "that's just my cunning; you remember I told you that the mermaid said that a mile further up the road—and by the road she means the river, for she can't go anywhere else—I should find another herd of cattle waiting for me. Well, I know how many bends there are in the river and what a roundabout way it would be. It's ever so

much shorter if you can come up on dry land and take the short cuts, you save a couple of miles by it, and get the cattle much sooner."

"Oh, you *are* a fortunate man!" said Great Claus; "do you think I should get some sea-cattle if I were to go down to the bottom of the river?"

"I'm sure you would," said Little Claus; "but I can't carry you in the sack to the river, you're too heavy for me. If you like to walk there and then get into the sack, I'll throw you into the river with the greatest pleasure in the world."

"Thank you," said Great Claus; "but if I don't get any sea-cattle when I get down there, see if I don't give you a sound thrashing."

"Oh! don't be so hard on me." They then walked off to the river. As soon as the cattle saw the water they rushed down to drink, for they were very thirsty. "See what a hurry they're in," said Little Claus; "they want to get down to the bottom again."

"Now help me first," said Great Claus, "or else I'll thrash you." He then crept into a big sack which had been lying across the back of one of the cows. "Put a big stone in, or I'm afraid I shan't sink," said Great Claus.

"Oh, that'll be all right," said Little Claus, but he put a big stone into the sack and gave it a push. Plump went the sack and Great Claus was in the river where he sank to the bottom at once.

"I'm afraid he won't find any cattle," said Little Claus, as he drove his herd home.

The Snow Queen

FIRST STORY

Deals with a mirror and its fragments. Now we are about
to begin, and you must attend; and when we get to the end
of the story, you will know more than you do now about a
very wicked hobgoblin. He was one of the worst kind; in
fact he was a real demon. One day he was in a high state of
delight, because he had invented a mirror with this peculiarity,
that every good and pretty thing reflected in it shrank away to
almost nothing. On the other hand, every bad and good-for-
nothing thing stood out and looked its worst. The most beautiful landscapes reflected in it looked like boiled spinach, and
the best people became hideous, or else they were upside
down and had no bodies. Their faces were distorted beyond
recognition, and if they had even one freckle it appeared to
spread all over the nose and mouth. The demon thought this
immensely amusing. If a good thought passed through anyone's mind, it turned to a grin in the mirror, and this caused
real delight to the demon. All the scholars of the demon's
school, for he kept a school, reported that a miracle had taken
place: now for the first time it had become possible to see what
the world and mankind were really like. They ran about all
over with the mirror, till at last there was not a country or a
person which had not been seen in this distorting mirror.
They even wanted to fly up to heaven with it to mock the angels;
but the higher they flew, the more it grinned, so much so that
they could hardly hold it, and at last it slipped out of their

hands and fell to the earth, shivered into hundreds of millions and billions of bits. Even then it did more harm than ever. Some of these bits were not as big as a grain of sand, and these flew about all over the world, getting into people's eyes, and, once in, they stuck there, and distorted everything they looked at, or made them see everything that was amiss. Each tiniest grain of glass kept the same power as that possessed by the whole mirror. Some people even got a bit of the glass into their hearts, and that was terrible, for the heart became like a lump of ice. Some of the fragments were so big that they were used for window panes, but it was not advisable to look at one's friends through these panes. Other bits were made into spectacles, and it was a bad business when people put on these spectacles meaning to be just. The bad demon laughed till he split his sides; it tickled him to see the mischief he had done. But some of these fragments were still left floating about the world, and you shall hear what happened to them.

About a Little Boy and a Little Girl

In a big town crowded with houses and people, where there is no room for gardens, people have to be content with flowers in pots instead. In one of these towns lived two children who managed to have something bigger than a flower-pot for a garden. They were not brother and sister, but they were just as fond of each other as if they had been. Their parents lived opposite each other in two attic rooms. The roof of one house just touched the roof of the next one, with only a rain water gutter between them. They each had a little dormer window, and one only had to step over the gutter to get from one house to the other. Each of the parents had a large window-box, in which they grew pot herbs and a little rose tree. There was one in each box, and they both grew splendidly. Then it occurred to the parents to put the boxes across the gutter, from house to house, and they looked just like two banks of flowers. The pea vines hung down over the edges of the boxes, and the roses threw out long creepers which twined round the windows. It was almost like a green triumphal arch. The boxes were high, and the children knew they must not climb up on to them, but they were often allowed to have their little stools out under the rose trees, and there they had delightful games. Of course in the winter there was an end to these amusements. The windows were often covered with hoar frost; then they would warm coppers on the stove and stick them on the frozen panes, where they made lovely peep-holes as round as possible. Then a bright eye would peep through these holes, one from each window. The little boy's name was Kay, and the little girl's Gerda.

In the summer they could reach each other with one bound, but in the winter they had to go down all the stairs in one house and up all the stairs in the other, and outside there were snowdrifts.

"Look! the white bees are swarming," said the old grandmother.

"Have they a queen bee too?" asked the little boy, for he knew that there was a queen among the real bees.

"Yes indeed they have," said the grandmother. "She flies where the swarm is thickest. She is the biggest of them all, and she never remains on the ground. She always flies up again to the sky. Many a winter's night she flies through the streets and peeps in at the windows, and then the ice freezes on the panes into wonderful patterns like flowers."

"Oh yes, we have seen that," said both children, and then they knew it was true.

"Can the Snow Queen come in here?" asked the little girl.

"Just let her come," said the boy, "and I will put her on the stove, where she will melt."

But the grandmother smoothed his hair and told him more stories.

In the evening when little Kay was at home and half undressed, he crept up on to the chair by the window, and peeped out of the little hole. A few snow-flakes were falling, and one of these, the biggest, remained on the edge of the window-box. It grew bigger and bigger, till it became the figure of a woman, dressed in the finest white gauze, which appeared to be made of millions of starry flakes. She was delicately lovely, but all ice, glittering, dazzling ice. Still she was alive, her eyes shone like two bright stars, but there was no rest or peace in them. She nodded to the window and waved her hand. The little boy was frightened and jumped down off the chair, and then he fancied that a big bird flew past the window.

The next day was bright and frosty, and then came the thaw—and after that the spring. The sun shone, green buds began to appear, the swallows built their nests, and people began to open their windows. The little children began to play in their garden on the roof again. The roses were in splendid bloom that summer; the little girl had learnt a hymn, and there was something in it about roses, and that made her think of her own. She sang it to the little boy, and then he sang it with her—

"Where roses deck the flowery vale,
There, Infant Jesus, we thee hail!"

The children took each other by the hands, kissed the roses and rejoiced in God's bright sunshine, and spoke to it as if the Child Jesus were there. What lovely summer days they were, and how delightful it was to sit out under the fresh rose trees, which seemed never tired of blooming.

Kay and Gerda were looking at a picture-book of birds and animals one day—it had just struck five by the church clock—when Kay said. "Oh, something struck my heart, and I have got something in my eye!"

The little girl put her arms round his neck, he blinked his eye, there was nothing to be seen.

"I believe it is gone," he said, but it was not gone. It was one of those very grains of glass from the mirror, the magic mirror. You remember that horrid mirror, in which all good and great things reflected in it became small and mean, while the bad things were magnified, and every flaw became very apparent.

Poor Kay! a grain of it had gone straight to his heart, and would soon turn it to a lump of ice. He did not feel it any more, but it was still there.

"Why do you cry?" he asked; "it makes you look ugly; there's nothing the matter with me. How horrid!" he suddenly cried; "there's a worm in that rose, and that one is quite crooked; after all, they are nasty roses, and so are the boxes they are growing in!" He kicked the box and broke off two of the roses.

"What are you doing, Kay?" cried the little girl. When he saw her alarm, he broke off another rose, and then ran in, by his own window, and left dear little Gerda alone.

When she next got out the picture-book he said it was only fit for babies in long clothes. When his grandmother told them stories he always had a but—, and if he could manage it, he liked to get behind her chair, put on her spectacles and imitate her. He did it very well, and people laughed at him. He was soon able to imitate every one in the street; he could make fun of all their peculiarities and failings. "He will turn out a clever fellow," said people. But it was all that bit of glass in his heart, that bit of glass in his eye, and it made him teaze little Gerda who was so devoted to him. He played quite different games now; he seemed to have grown older. One winter's day, when the snow was falling fast, he brought in a big magnifying glass; he held out the tail of his blue coat, and let the snow-flakes fall upon it.

"Now look through the glass, Gerda!" he said; every snow-flake was magnified, and looked like a lovely flower, or a sharply pointed star.

"Do you see how cleverly they are made," said Kay. "Much more interesting than looking at real flowers, and there is not a single flaw in them, they are perfect, if only they would not melt."

Shortly after, he appeared in his thick gloves, with his sledge on his back. He shouted right into Gerda's ear, "I have got leave to drive in the big square where the other boys play!" and away he went.

In the big square the bolder boys used to tie their little sledges to the farm carts and go a long way in this fashion. They had no end of fun over it. Just in the middle of their games, a big sledge came along; it was painted white, and the occupant wore a white fur coat and cap. The sledge drove twice round the square, and Kay quickly tied his sledge on behind. Then off they went, faster and faster, into the next street. The driver turned round and nodded to Kay in the most friendly way, just as if they knew each other. Every time Kay wanted to loose his sledge, the person nodded again, and Kay stayed where he was, and they drove right out through the town gates. Then the snow began to fall so heavily that the little boy could not see a hand before him as they rushed along. He undid the cords, and tried to get away from the big sledge, but it was no use, his little sledge stuck fast, and on they rushed, faster than the wind. He shouted aloud, but nobody heard him, and the sledge tore on through the snowdrifts. Every now and then it gave a bound, as if they were jumping over hedges and ditches. He was very frightened, and he wanted to say his prayers, but he could only remember the multiplication tables.

The snow-flakes grew bigger and bigger, till at last they looked like big white chickens. All at once they sprang on one side, the big sledge stopped, and the person who drove got up, coat and cap smothered in snow. It was a tall and upright lady all shining white, the Snow Queen herself.

"We have come along at a good pace," she said; "but it's cold enough to kill one; creep inside my bearskin coat."

She took him into the sledge by her, wrapped him in her furs, and he felt as if he were sinking into a snowdrift.

"Are you still cold?" she asked, and she kissed him on the forehead. Ugh! it was colder than ice, it went to his very heart, which was already more than half ice; he felt as if he were dying, but only for a moment, and then it seemed to have done him good, he no longer felt the cold.

"My sledge! don't forget my sledge!" He only remembered it now, it was tied to one of the white chickens which flew along behind them. The Snow Queen kissed Kay again, and then he forgot all about little Gerda, Grandmother, and all the others at home.

"Now I mustn't kiss you any more," she said "or I should kiss you to death!"

Kay looked at her, she was so pretty; a cleverer, more beautiful face could hardly be imagined. She did not seem to be made of ice now, as she was outside the window when she waved her hand to him. In his eyes she was quite perfect, and he was not a bit afraid of her; he told her that he could do mental arithmetic, as far as fractions, and that he knew the number of square miles and the number of inhabitants of the country. She always smiled at him, and he then thought that he surely did not know enough, and he looked up into the wide expanse of heaven, into which they rose higher and higher as she flew with him on a dark cloud, while the storm surged around them, the wind ringing in their ears like well-known old songs.

They flew over woods and lakes, over oceans and islands, the cold wind whistled down below them, the wolves howled, the black crows flew screaming over the sparkling snow, but up above, the moon shone bright and clear—and Kay looked at it all the long, long winter nights; in the day he slept at the Snow Queen's feet.

The Garden of the Woman Learned in Magic

But how was little Gerda getting on all this long time since Kay left her? Where could he be? Nobody knew, nobody could say anything about him. All that the other boys knew was, that they had seen him tie his little sledge to a splendid big one which drove away down the street and out of the town gates. Nobody knew where he was, and many tears were shed; little Gerda cried long and bitterly. At last, people said he was dead; he must have fallen into the river which ran close by the town. Oh, what long, dark, winter days those were!

At last the spring came and the sunshine.

"Kay is dead and gone," said Little Gerda.

"I don't believe it," said the sunshine.

"He is dead and gone," she said to the swallows.

"We don't believe it," said the swallows, and at last little Gerda did not believe it either.

"I will put on my new red shoes," she said one morning; "those Kay never saw; and then I will go down to the river and ask it about him!"

It was very early in the morning; she kissed the old grandmother, who was still asleep, put on the red shoes, and went quite alone, out by the gate to the river.

"Is it true that you have taken my little playfellow? I will give you my red shoes if you will bring him back to me."

She thought the little ripples nodded in such a curious

way, so she took off her red shoes, her most cherished possessions, and threw them both into the river. They fell close by the shore, and were carried straight back to her by the little wavelets; it seemed as if the river would not accept her offering, as it had not taken little Kay.

She only thought she had not thrown them far enough, so she climbed into a boat which lay among the rushes, then she went right out to the further end of it, and threw the shoes into the water again. But the boat was loose, and her movements started it off, and it floated away from the shore: she felt it moving and tried to get out, but before she reached the other end the boat was more than a yard from the shore, and was floating away quite quickly.

Little Gerda was terribly frightened, and began to cry, but nobody heard her except the sparrows, and they could not carry her ashore, but they flew alongside twittering as if to cheer her, "We are here, we are here." The boat floated rapidly away with the current; little Gerda sat quite still with only her stockings on; her little red shoes floated behind, but they could not catch up the boat which drifted away faster and faster.

The banks on both sides were very pretty with beautiful flowers, fine old trees, and slopes dotted with sheep and cattle, but not a single person.

"Perhaps the river is taking me to little Kay," thought Gerda, and that cheered her; she sat up and looked at the beautiful green banks for hours.

Then they came to a big cherry garden; there was a little house in it, with curious blue and red windows, it had a thatched roof, and two wooden soldiers stood outside, who presented arms as she sailed past. Gerda called out to them;

she thought they were alive, but of course they did not answer; she was quite close to them, for the current drove the boat close to the bank. Gerda called out again, louder than before, and then an old, old woman came out of the house; she was leaning upon a big, hooked stick, and she wore a big sun hat, which was covered with beautiful painted flowers.

"You poor little child," said the old woman, "however were you driven out on this big, strong river into the wide, wide, world alone?" Then she walked right into the water, and caught hold of the boat with her hooked stick; she drew it ashore, and lifted little Gerda out.

Gerda was delighted to be on dry land again, but she was a little bit frightened of the strange old woman.

"Come, tell me who you are, and how you got here," said she.

When Gerda had told her the whole story, and asked her if she had seen Kay, the woman said she had not seen him, but that she expected him. Gerda must not be sad, she was to come and taste her cherries and see her flowers, which were more beautiful than any picture-book; each one had a story to tell. Then she took Gerda by the hand, they went into the little house, and the old woman locked the door.

The windows were very high up, and they were red, blue, and yellow; they threw a very curious light into the room. On the table were quantities of the most delicious cherries, of which Gerda had leave to eat as many as ever she liked. While she was eating, the old woman combed her hair with a golden comb, so that her hair curled, and shone like gold round the pretty little face, which was as sweet as a rose.

"I have long wanted a little girl like you!" said the old woman. "You will see how well we shall get on together."

While she combed her hair Gerda had forgotten all about Kay, for the old woman was learned in the magic art, but she was not a bad witch, she only cast spells over people for a little amusement, and she wanted to keep Gerda. She therefore went into the garden and waved her hooked stick over all the rose-bushes, and however beautifully they were flowering, all sank down into the rich black earth without leaving a trace behind them. The old woman was afraid that if Gerda saw the roses she would be reminded of Kay, and would want to run away. Then she took Gerda into the flower-garden. What a delicious scent there was! and every imaginable flower for every season was in that lovely garden; no picture-book could be brighter or more beautiful. Gerda jumped for joy and played till the sun went down behind the tall cherry trees. Then she was put into a lovely bed with rose coloured silken coverings stuffed with violets; she slept and dreamt as lovely dreams as any queen on her wedding day.

The next day she played with the flowers in the garden again —and many days passed in the same way. Gerda knew every flower, but however many there were, she always thought there was one missing, but which it was she did not know.

One day she was sitting looking at the old woman's sun hat with its painted flowers, and the very prettiest one of them all was a rose. The old woman had forgotten her hat when she charmed the others away. This is the consequence of being absent-minded.

"What!" said Gerda, "are there no roses here?" and she sprang in among the flower beds and sought, but in vain! Her hot tears fell on the very places where the roses used to be; when the warm drops moistened the earth, the rose trees shot up again just as full of bloom as when they sank. Gerda embraced the roses and kissed them, and then she thought of the lovely roses at home, and this brought the thought of little Kay.

"Oh, how I have been delayed," said the little girl, "I ought to have been looking for Kay! Don't you know where he is?" she asked the roses. "Do you think he is dead and gone?"

"He is not dead," said the roses. "For we have been down underground, you know, and all the dead people are there, but Kay is not among them."

"Oh, thank you!" said little Gerda, and then she went to the other flowers and looked into their cups and said, "Do you know where Kay is?"

But each flower stood in the sun and dreamt its own dreams. Little Gerda heard many of these, but never anything about Kay.

And what said the Tiger lilies?

"Do you hear the drum? rub-a-dub, it has only two notes, rub-a-dub, always the same. The wailing of women and the cry of the preacher. The Hindu woman in her long red garment stands on the pile, while the flames surround her and her dead husband. But the woman is only thinking of the living man in the circle round, whose eyes burn with a fiercer fire than that of the flames which consume the body. Do the flames of the heart die in the fire?"

"I understand nothing about that," said little Gerda.

"That is my story," said the Tiger lily.

"What does the convolvulus say?"

"An old castle is perched high over a narrow mountain path, it is closely covered with ivy, almost hiding the old red walls, and creeping up leaf upon leaf right round the balcony where stands a beautiful maiden. She bends over the balustrade and looks eagerly up the road. No rose on its stem is fresher than she; no apple blossom wafted by the wind moves more lightly. Her silken robes rustle softly as she bends over and says, "Will he never come?"

"Is it Kay you mean?" asked Gerda.

"I am only talking about my own story, my dream," answered the convolvulus.

What said the little snowdrop?

"Between two trees a rope with a board is hanging; it is a swing. Two pretty little girls in snowy frocks and green ribbons fluttering on their hats are seated on it. Their brother, who is bigger than they are, stands up behind them; he has his arms round the ropes for supports, and holds in one hand a little bowl and in the other a clay pipe. He is blowing soap-bubbles. As the swing moves the bubbles fly upwards in all their changing colours, the last one still hangs from the pipe swayed by the wind, and the swing goes on. A little black dog runs up, he is almost as light as the bubbles, he stands up on his hind legs and wants to be taken into the swing, but it does not stop. The little dog falls with an angry bark, they jeer at it; the bubble bursts. A swinging plank, a fluttering foam picture—that is my story!"

"I daresay what you tell me is very pretty, but you speak so sadly, and you never mention little Kay."

What says the hyacinth?

"They were three beautiful sisters, all most delicate, and quite transparent. One wore a crimson robe, the other a blue, and the third was pure white. These three danced hand-in-hand, by the edge of the lake in the moonlight. They were human beings, not fairies of the wood. The fragrant air attracted them, and they vanished into the wood; here the fragrance was stronger still. Three coffins glide out of the wood towards the lake, and in them lie the maidens. The fireflies flutter lightly round them with their little flickering torches. Do these dancing maidens sleep, or are they dead? The scent of the flower says that they are corpses. The evening bell tolls their knell."

"You make me quite sad," said little Gerda; "your perfume is so strong it makes me think of those dead maidens. Oh, is little Kay really dead? The roses have been down underground, and they say no."

"Ding, dong," tolled the hyacinth bells; "we are not tolling for little Kay; we know nothing about him. We sing our song, the only one we know."

And Gerda went on to the buttercups shining among their dark green leaves.

"You are a bright little sun," said Gerda. "Tell me if you know where I shall find my playfellow."

The buttercup shone brightly and returned Gerda's glance. What song could the buttercup sing? It would not be about Kay.

"God's bright sun shone into a little court on the first day of spring. The sunbeams stole down the neighbouring white wall, close to which bloomed the first yellow flower of the season; it shone like burnished gold in the sun. An old woman had brought her arm-chair out into the sun; her granddaughter, a poor and pretty little maid-servant, had come to pay her a short visit, and she kissed her. There was gold, heart's gold, in the kiss. Gold on the lips, gold on the ground, and gold above, in the early morning beams! Now that is my little story," said the buttercup.

"Oh, my poor old grandmother!" sighed Gerda. "She will be longing to see me, and grieving about me, as she did about Kay. But I shall soon go home again and take Kay with me. It is useless for me to ask the flowers about him. They only know their own stories, and have no information to give me."

Then she tucked up her little dress, so that she might run the faster, but the narcissus blossoms struck her on the legs as she jumped over them, so she stopped and said, "Perhaps you can tell me something."

She stooped down close to the flower and listened. What did it say?

"I can see myself, I can see myself," said the narcissus. "Oh, how sweet is my scent. Up there in an attic window stands a little dancing girl half dressed; first she stands on one leg, then on the other, and looks as if she would tread the whole world under her feet. She is only a delusion. She pours some water out of a teapot on to a bit of stuff that she is holding; it is her bodice. 'Cleanliness is a good thing, she says.' Her white dress hangs on a peg; it has been washed in the teapot, too, and dried on the roof. She puts it on, and wraps a saffron coloured scarf round her neck, which makes the dress look whiter. See how high she carries her head, and all upon one stem. I see myself, I see myself!"

"I don't care a bit about all that," said Gerda; "it's no use telling me such stuff."

And then she ran to the end of the garden. The door was fastened, but she pressed the rusty latch, and it gave way. The door sprang open, and little Gerda ran out with bare feet into the wide world. She looked back three times, but nobody came after her. At last she could run no further, and she sat down on a big stone. When she looked round she saw that the summer was over, it was quite late autumn. She would never have known it inside the beautiful garden, where the sun always shone and the flowers of every season were always in bloom.

"Oh, how I have wasted my time," said little Gerda. "It is autumn. I must not rest any longer," and she got up to go on.

Oh, how weary and sore were her little feet, and everything round looked so cold and dreary. The long willow leaves were quite yellow. The damp mist fell off the trees like rain, one leaf dropped after another from the trees, and only the sloe-thorn still bore its fruit, but the sloes were sour and set one's teeth on edge. Oh, how grey and sad it looked, out in the wide world.

FOURTH STORY

Prince and Princess

Gerda was soon obliged to rest again. A big crow hopped on to the snow, just in front of her. It had been sitting looking at her for a long time and wagging its head. Now it said "Caw, caw; good-day, good-day," as well as it could; it meant to be kind to the little girl, and asked her where she was going, alone in the wide world.

Gerda understood the word "alone" and knew how much there was in it, and she told the crow the whole story of her life and adventures, and asked if it had seen Kay.

The crow nodded his head gravely and said, "May be I have, may be I have."

"What, do you really think you have?" cried the little girl, nearly smothering him with her kisses.

"Gently, gently!" said the crow. "I believe it may have been Kay, but he has forgotten you by this time, I expect, for the Princess."

"Does he live with a Princess?" asked Gerda.

"Yes, listen," said the crow; "but it is so difficult to speak your language. If you understand 'crow's language,'[1] I can tell you about it much better."

"No, I have never learnt it," said Gerda; "but grandmother knew it, and used to speak it. If only I had learnt it!"

---

[1] Children have a kind of language, or of gibberish, formed by adding letters or syllables to every word, which is called "crow's language."

"It doesn't matter," said the crow. "I will tell you as well as I can, although I may do it rather badly."

Then he told her what he had heard.

"In this kingdom where we are now," said he, "there lives a Princess who is very clever. She has read all the newspapers in the world, and forgotten them again, so clever is she. One day she was sitting on her throne, which is not such an amusing thing to do either, they say; and she began humming a tune, which happened to be

'Why should I not be married, oh why?'

'Why not indeed?' said she. And she made up her mind to marry, if she could find a husband who had an answer ready when a question was put to him. She called all the court ladies together, and when they heard what she wanted, they were delighted.

" 'I like that now,' they said. 'I was thinking the same thing myself the other day."

"Every word I say is true," said the crow, "for I have a tame sweetheart who goes about the Palace whenever she likes. She told me the story."

Of course his sweetheart was a crow, for "birds of a feather flock together," and one crow always chooses another. The newspapers all came out immediately with borders of hearts and the Princess's initials. They gave notice that any young man who was handsome enough might go up to the Palace to speak to the Princess. The one who spoke as if he were quite at home, and spoke well, would be chosen by the Princess as her husband. Yes, yes, you may believe me, it's as true as I sit here," said the crow. "The people came crowding in; there was such running, and crushing, but no one was fortunate enough to be chosen, either on the first day, or on the second. They could all of them talk well enough in the street, but when they entered the castle gates, and saw the guard in silver uniforms, and when they went up the stairs through rows of lackeys in gold embroidered liveries, their courage forsook them. When they reached the brilliantly lighted reception rooms, and stood in front of the throne where the Princess was seated, they could think of nothing to say, they only echoed her last words, and of course that was not what she wanted.

It was just as if they had all taken some kind of sleeping powder, which made them lethargic; they did not recover themselves until they got out into the street again, and then they had plenty to say. There was quite a long line of them, reaching from the town gates up to the Palace.

"I went to see them myself," said the crow. "They were hungry and thirsty, but they got nothing at the Palace, not even as much as a glass of tepid water. Some of the wise ones had taken sandwiches with them, but they did not share them with their neighbours; they thought if the others went in to the Princess looking hungry, that there would be more chance for themselves."

"But Kay, little Kay!" asked Gerda; "when did he come? was he amongst the crowd?"

"Give me time, give me time! we are just coming to him. It was on the third day that a little personage came marching cheerfully along, without either carriage or horse. His eyes sparkled like yours, and he had beautiful long hair, but his clothes were very shabby."

"Oh, that was Kay!" said Gerda gleefully; "then I have found him!" and she clapped her hands.

"He had a little knapsack on his back!" said the crow.

"No, it must have been his sledge; he had it with him when he went away!" said Gerda.

"It may be so," said the crow; "I did not look very particularly! but I know from my sweetheart, that when he entered the Palace gates, and saw the life guards in the silver uniforms, and the lackeys on the stairs in their gold laced liveries, he was not the least bit abashed. He just nodded to them and said, 'It must be very tiresome to stand upon the stairs. I am going inside!' The rooms were blazing with lights. Privy councillors and excellencies without number were walking about barefoot carrying golden vessels; it was enough to make you solemn! His boots creaked fearfully too, but he wasn't a bit upset."

"Oh, I am sure that was Kay!" said Gerda; "I know he had a pair of news boots, I heard them creaking in grandmother's room."

"Yes, indeed they did creak!" said the crow. "But nothing daunted, he went straight up to the Princess, who was sitting on a pearl, as big as a spinning-wheel. Poor, simple boy! all the court ladies and their attendants; the courtiers, and their gentlemen, each attended by a page, were standing round. The nearer the door they stood, so much the greater was their haughtiness; till the footman's boy who always wore slippers and stood in the doorway, was almost too proud even to be looked at."

"It must be awful!" said little Gerda, "and yet Kay has won the Princess!"

"If I had not been a crow, I should have taken her myself, notwithstanding that I am engaged. They say he spoke as well as I could have done myself, when I speak crow-language; at least so my sweetheart says. He was a picture of good looks and gallantry, and then he had not come with any idea of wooing the Princess, but simply to hear her wisdom. He admired her just as much as she admired him!"

"Indeed it was Kay then," said Gerda; "he was so clever he could do mental arithmetic up to fractions. Oh won't you take me to the Palace?"

"It's easy enough to talk," said the crow; "but how are we to manage it? I will talk to my tame sweetheart about it; she will have some advice to give us I daresay, but I am bound to tell you that a little girl like you will never be admitted!"

"Oh, indeed I shall," said Gerda; "when Kay hears that I am here, he will come out at once to fetch me."

"Wait here for me by the stile," said the crow, then he wagged his head and flew off.

The evening had darkened in before he came back. "Caw, caw," he said, "she sends you greeting, and here is a little roll for you, she got it out of the kitchen where there is bread enough, and I daresay you are hungry! It is not possible for you to get into the Palace, you have bare feet, the guards in silver and the lackeys in gold would never allow you to pass. But don't cry, we shall get you in somehow; my sweetheart knows a little back staircase which leads up to the bedroom, and she knows where the key is kept."

Then they went into the garden, into the great avenue where the leaves were, softly one by one; and when the Palace lights went out, one after the other, the crow led little Gerda to the back door, which was ajar.

Oh, how Gerda's heart beat with fear and longing! It was just as if she was about to do something wrong, and yet she only wanted to know if this really was little Kay. Oh, it must be him, she thought picturing to herself his clever eyes and his

long hair. She could see his very smile when they used to sit
under the rose trees at home. She thought he would be very
glad to see her, and to hear what a long way she had come to
find him, and to hear how sad they had all been at home when
he did not come back. Oh, it was joy mingled with fear.

They had now reached the stairs, where a little lamp was
burning on a shelf. There stood the tame sweetheart, twisting
and turning her head to look at Gerda, who made a curtsey, as
grandmother had taught her.

"My betrothed has spoken so charmingly to me about you,
my little miss!" she said; "your life, '*Vita,*' as it is called, is
most touching! If you will take the lamp, I will go on in front.
We shall take the straight road here, and we shall meet no
one."

"It seems to me that someone is coming up behind us,"
said Gerda, as she fancied something rushed past her throwing
a shadow on the walls; horses with flowing manes and slender
legs; huntsmen, ladies and gentlemen, on horseback.

"Oh, those are only the dreams!" said the crow; "they come
to take the thoughts of the noble ladies and gentlemen out
hunting. That's a good thing, for you will be able to see them
all the better in bed. But don't forget, when you are taken
into favour, that you show a grateful spirit."

"Now, there's no need to talk about that," said the crow
from the woods.

They now came into the first apartment; it was hung with
rose-coloured satin embroidered with flowers. Here again the
dreams overtook them, but they flitted by so quickly that
Gerda could not distinguish them. The apartments became
one more beautiful than the other; they were enough to
bewilder anybody. They now reached the bedroom. The

ceiling was like a great palm with crystal leaves, and in the middle of the room two beds, each like a lily hung from a golden stem. One was white, and in it lay the Princess; the other was red, and there lay he whom Gerda had come to seek—little Kay! She bent aside one of the crimson leaves, and she saw a little brown neck. It was Kay! She called his name aloud, and held the lamp close to him. Again the dreams rushed through the room on horseback—he awoke, turned his head—and it was not little Kay. It was only the Prince's neck which was like his; but he was young and handsome. The princess peeped out of her lily-white bed, and asked what was the matter. Then little Gerda cried and told them all her story, and what the crows had done to help her.

"You poor little thing!" said the Prince and Princess. And they praised the crows, and said that they were not all at angry with them, but they must not do it again. Then they gave them a reward.

"Would you like your liberty?" said the Princess, "or would you prefer permanent posts about the court as court crows with perquisites from the kitchen?"

Both crows curtsied and begged for the permanent posts, for they thought of their old age, and said "it was so good to have something for the old man," as they called it.

The Prince got up and allowed Gerda to sleep in his bed, and he could not have done more. She folded her little hands and thought "how good the people and the animals are:" then she shut her eyes and fell fast asleep. All the dreams came flying back again; this time they looked like angels, and they were dragging a little sledge with Kay sitting on it, and he nodded. But it was only a dream; so it all vanished when she woke.

Next day she was dressed in silk and velvet from head to foot; they asked her to stay at the Palace and have a good time, but she only begged them to give her a little carriage and horse, and a little pair of boots, so that she might drive out into the wide world to look for Kay.

They gave her a pair of boots and a muff. She was beautifully dressed, and when she was ready to start, there before the door stood a new chariot of pure gold. The Prince's and Princess's coat of arms were emblazoned on it, and shone like a star. Coachman, footman, and outrider, for there was even an outrider, all wore golden crowns. The Prince and Princess themselves helped her into the carriage and wished her joy. The wood crow, who was now married, accompanied her for the first three miles, he sat beside Gerda, for he could not ride with his back to the horses; the other crow stood at the door and flapped her wings, she did not go with them, for she suffered from headache since she had been a kitchen pensioner—the consequence of eating too much. The chariot was stored with sugar biscuits, and there were fruit and ginger nuts under the seat. "Good-bye, good-bye," cried the Prince and Princess; little Gerda wept and the crow wept too. At the end of the first few miles the crow said good-bye, and this was the hardest parting of all. It flew up into a tree and flapped its big black wings as long as it could see the chariot which shone like the brightest sunshine.

The Little Robber Girl

They drove on through a dark wood, where the chariot lighted up the way and blinded the robbers by its glare; it was more than they could bear.

"It is gold, it is gold!" they cried, and darting forward, feized the horses, and killed the postilions, the coachman, and sootman. They then dragged little Gerda out of the carriage.

"She is fat, and she is pretty, she has been fattened on nuts!" said the old robber woman, who had a long beard, and eyebrows that hung down over her eyes. "She is as good as a fat lamb, and how nice she will taste!" She drew out her sharp knife as she said this; it glittered horribly. "Oh!" screamed the old woman at the same moment, for her little daughter had come up behind her, and she was biting her ear. She hung on her back, as wild and as savage a little animal as you could wish to find. "You bad, wicked child!" said the mother, but she was prevented from killing Gerda on this occasion.

"She shall play with me," said the little robber girl; "she shall give me her muff, and her pretty dress, and she shall sleep in my bed." Then she bit her mother again and made her dance. All the robbers laughed and said, "Look at her dancing with her cub!"

"I want to get into the carriage," said the little robber girl, and she always had her own way, because she was so spoilt and stubborn. She and Gerda got into the carriage, and then they drove over stubble and stones further and further into the wood. The little robber girl was as big as Gerda, but much stronger; she had broader shoulders, and darker skin, her eyes were quite black, with almost a melancholy expression. She put her arm round Gerda's waist and said,—

"They shan't kill you as long as I don't get angry with you; you must surely be a Princess!"

"No," said little Gerda, and then she told her all her adventures, and how fond she was of Kay.

The robber girl looked earnestly at her, gave a little nod, and said, "They shan't kill you even if I am angry with you. I will do it myself." Then she dried Gerda's eyes, and stuck her own hands into the pretty muff, which was so soft and warm.

At last the chariot stopped; they were in the courtyard of a robber's castle, the walls of which were cracked from top to bottom. Ravens and crows flew in and out of every hole, and big bull-dogs, which each looked ready to devour somebody, jumped about as high as they could, but they did not bark, for it was not allowed. A big fire was burning in the middle of the stone floor of the smoky old hall. The smoke all went up to the ceiling where it had to find a way out for itself. Soup was boiling in a big cauldron over the fire, and hares and rabbits were roasting on the spits.

"You shall sleep with me and all my little pets to-night," said the robber girl.

When they had had something to eat and drink they went along to one corner which was spread with straw and rugs. There were nearly a hundred pigeons roosting overhead on the rafters and beams. They seemed to be asleep, but they fluttered about a little when the children came in.

"They are all mine," said the little robber girl, seizing one of the nearest. She held it by the legs and shook it till it flapped its wings. "Kiss it," she cried, dashing it at Gerda's face. "Those are the wood pigeons," she added, pointing to some laths fixed across a big hole high up on the walls; "they are a regular rabble; they would fly away directly if they were not locked in. And here is my old sweetheart Be," dragging forward a reindeer by the horn; it was tied up, and it had a bright copper ring round its neck. "We have to keep him close too, or he would run off. Every single night I tickle his neck with my bright knife, he is so frightened of it." The little girl produced a long knife out of a hole in the wall and drew it across the reindeer's neck. The poor animal laughed and kicked, and the robber girl laughed and pulled Gerda down into the bed with her.

"Do you have that knife by you while you are asleep?" asked Gerda, looking rather frightened.

"I always sleep with a knife," said the little robber girl. "You never know what will happen. But now tell me again what you told me before about little Kay, and why you went out into the world." So Gerda told her all about it again, and the wood pigeons cooed up in their cage above them, the other pigeons were asleep. The little robber girl put her arm round Gerda's neck and went to sleep with the knife in her other hand, and she was soon snoring. But Gerda would not close her eyes; she did not know whether she was to live or to die. The robbers sat round the fire, eating and drinking, and the old woman was turning somersaults. This sight terrified the poor little girl. Then the wood pigeons said, "Coo, coo, we have seen little Kay, his sledge was drawn by a white chicken and he was sitting in the Snow Queen's sledge; it was floating low down over the trees, while we were in our nests. She blew upon us young ones, and they all died except we two; coo, coo."

"What are you saying up there?" asked Gerda. "Where was the Snow Queen going? Do you know anything about it?"

"She was most likely going to Lapland, because there is always snow and ice there! Ask the reindeer who is tied up there."

"There is ice and snow, and it's a splendid place," said the reindeer. "You can run and jump about where you like on those big glittering plains. The Snow Queen has her summer tent there, but her permanent castle is up at the North Pole, on the island which is called Spitzbergen!"

"Oh Kay, little Kay!" sighed Gerda.

"Lie still, or I shall stick the knife into you!" said the robber girl.

In the morning Gerda told her all that the wood pigeons had said, and the little robber girl looked quite solemn, but she nodded her head and said, "No matter, no matter! Do you know where Lapland is?" she asked the reindeer.

"Who should know better than I," said the animal, its eyes dancing. "I was born and brought up there, and I used to leap about on the snow-fields."

"Listen," said the robber girl. "You see that all our men folks are away, but mother is still here, and she will stay; but later on in the morning she will take a drink out of the big bottle there, and after that she will have a nap—then I will do something for you." Then she jumped out of bed, ran along to her mother and pulled her beard, and said, "Good-morning, my own dear nanny-goat!" And her mother filliped her nose till it was red and blue; but it was all affection.

As soon as her mother had had her draught from the bottle and had dropped asleep, the little robber girl went along to the reindeer, and said, "I should have the greatest pleasure in the world in keeping you here, to tickle you with my knife, because you are such fun then; however, it does not matter. I will untie your halter and help you outside so that you may run away to Lapland, but you must put your best foot foremost, and take this little girl for me to the Snow Queen's palace, where her playfellow is. I have no doubt you heard what she was telling me, for she spoke loud enough, and you are generally eavesdropping!"

The reindeer jumped into the air for joy. The robber girl lifted little Gerda up, and had the forethought to tie her on, nay, even to give her a little cushion to sit upon. "Here, after all, I will give you your fur boots back, for it will be very cold, but I will keep your muff, it is too pretty to part with. Still you shan't be cold. Here are my mother's big mittens for you, they will reach up to your elbows; here, stick your hands in! Now your hands look just like my nasty mother's."

Gerda shed tears of joy.

"I don't like you to whimper!" said the little robber girl. "You ought to be looking delighted; and here are two loaves and a ham for you, so that you shan't starve."

These things were tied on to the back of the reindeer; the little robber girl opened the door, called in all the big dogs, and then she cut the halter with her knife, and said to the reindeer, "Now run, but take care of my little girl!"

Gerda stretched out her hands in the big mittens to the robber girl and said good-bye; and then the reindeer darted off over briars and bushes, through the big wood, over swamps and plains, as fast as it could go. The wolves howled and the ravens screamed, while the red lights quivered up in the sky.

"There are my old northern lights," said the reindeer; "see how they flash!" and on it rushed faster than ever, day and night. The loaves were eaten, and the ham too, and then they were in Lapland.

The Lapp Woman and the Finn Woman

They stopped by a little hut, a very poverty-stricken one; the roof sloped right down to the ground, and the door was so low that the people had to creep on hands and knees when they wanted to go in or out. There was nobody at home here but an old Lapp woman, who was frying fish over a train-oil lamp. The reindeer told her all Gerda's story, but it told its own first; for it thought it was much the most important. Gerda was so overcome by the cold that she could not speak at all.

"Oh you poor creatures!" said the Lapp woman; "you've got a long way to go yet; you will have to go hundreds of miles into Finmark, for the Snow Queen is paying a country visit there, and she burns blue lights every night. I will write a few words on a dried stock-fish, for I have no paper. I will give it to you to take to the Finn woman up there. She will be better able to direct you than I can."

So when Gerda was warmed, and had eaten and drunk something, the Lapp woman wrote a few words on a dried stock-fish and gave it to her, bidding her take good care of it. Then she tied her on to the reindeer again, and off they flew. Flicker, flicker, went the beautiful blue northern lights up in the sky all night long;—at last they came to Finmark, and knocked on the Finn woman's chimney, for she had no door at all.

There was such a heat inside that the Finn woman went about almost naked; she was little and very grubby. She at once loosened Gerda's things, and took off the mittens and the boots, or she would have been too hot. Then she put a piece of ice on the reindeer's head, and after that she read what was written on the stock-fish. She read it three times, and then she knew it by heart, and put the fish into the pot for dinner; there was no reason why it should not be eaten, and she never wasted anything.

Again the reindeer told his own story first, and then little Gerda's. The Finn woman blinked with her wise eyes, but she said nothing.

"You are so clever," said the reindeer, "I know you can bind all the winds of the world with a bit of sewing cotton. When a skipper unties one knot he gets a good wind, when he unties two it blows hard, and if he undoes the third and the fourth he brings a storm about his head wild enough to blow down the forest trees. Won't you give the little girl a drink, so that she may have the strength of twelve men to overcome the Snow Queen?"

"The strength of twelve men," said the Finn woman. "Yes, that will be about enough."

She went along to a shelf and took down a big folded skin, which she unrolled. There were curious characters written on it, and the Finn woman read till the perspiration poured down her forehead.

But the reindeer again implored her to give Gerda something, and Gerda looked at her with such beseeching eyes, full of tears, that the Finn woman began blinking again, and drew the reindeer along into a corner, where she whispered to it, at the same time putting fresh ice on its head.

"Little Kay is certainly with the Snow Queen, and he is delighted with everything there. He thinks it is the best place in the world, but that is because he has got a splinter of glass in his heart and a grain of glass in his eye. They will have to come out first, or he will never be human again, and the Snow Queen will keep him in her power!"

"But can't you give little Gerda something to take which will give her power to conquer it all?"

"I can't give her greater power than she already has. Don't you see how great it is? Don't you see how both man and beast have to serve her? How she has got on as well as she has on her bare feet? We must not tell her what power she has; it is in her heart, because she is such a sweet innocent child. If she can't reach the Snow Queen herself, then we can't help her. The Snow Queen's gardens begin just two miles from here; you can carry the little girl as far as that. Put her down by the big bush standing there in the snow covered with red berries. Don't stand gossiping, but hurry back to me!" Then the Finn woman lifted Gerda on to the reindeer's back, and it rushed off as hard as it could.

"Oh, I have not got my boots, and I have not got my mittens!" cried little Gerda.

She soon felt the want of them in that cutting wind, but the reindeer did not dare to stop. It ran on till it came to the bush with the red berries. There it put Gerda down, and kissed her on the mouth, while big shining tears trickled down its face. Then it ran back again as fast as ever it could. There stood poor little Gerda, without shoes or gloves, in the middle of freezing icebound Finmark.

She ran forward as quickly as she could. A whole regiment of snow-flakes came towards her; they did not fall from the sky, for it was quite clear, with the northern lights shining brightly. No; these snow-flakes ran along the ground, and the nearer they came the bigger they grew. Gerda remembered well how big and ingenious they looked under the magnifying glass. But the size of these was monstrous, they were alive, they were the Snow Queen's advanced guard, and they took the most curious shapes. Some looked like big, horrid porcupines, some like bundles of knotted snakes with their heads sticking out. Others, again, were like fat little bears with bristling hair but all were dazzling white and living snow-flakes.

Then little Gerda said the Lord's Prayer, and the cold was so great that her breath froze as it came out of her mouth and she could see it like a cloud of smoke in front of her. It grew thicker and thicker, till it formed itself into bright little angels who grew bigger and bigger when they touched the ground. They all wore helmets and carried shields and spears in their hands. More and more of them appeared, and when Gerda had finished her prayer she was surrounded by a whole legion. They pierced the snow-flakes with their spears and shivered them into a hundred pieces, and little Gerda walked fearlessly and undauntedly through them. The angels touched her hands and her feet, and then she hardly felt how cold it was, but walked quickly on towards the Palace of the Snow Queen.

Now we must see what Kay was about. He was not thinking about Gerda at all, least of all that she was just outside the Palace.

What Happened at the Snow Queen's Palace and Afterwards

The Palace walls were made of drifted snow, and the windows and doors of the biting winds. There were over a hundred rooms in it, shaped just as the snow had drifted. The biggest one stretched for many miles. They were all lighted by the strongest northern lights. All the rooms were immensely big and empty, and glittering in their iciness. There was never any gaiety in them; not even so much as a ball for the little bears, when the storms might have turned up as the orchestra, and the polar bears might have walked about on their hind legs and shown off their grand manners. There was never even a little game-playing party, for such games as "touch last" or "the biter bit"—no, not even a little gossip over the coffee cups for the white fox misses. Immense, vast, and cold were the Snow Queen's halls. The northern lights came and went with such regularity that you could count the seconds between their coming and going. In the midst of these never-ending snow-halls was a frozen lake. It was broken up on the surface into a thousand bits, but each piece was so exactly like the others that the whole formed a perfect work of art. The Snow Queen sat in the very middle of it when she sat at home. She then said that she was sitting on "The Mirror of Reason," and that it was the best and only one in the world.

Little Kay was blue with cold, nay, almost black; but he did not know it, for the Snow Queen had kissed away the icy shiverings, and his heart was little better than a lump of ice. He went about dragging some sharp, flat pieces of ice, which he placed in all sorts of patterns, trying to make something out of them; just as when we at home have little tablets of wood, with which we make patterns, and call them a "Chinese puzzle."

Kay's patterns were most ingenious, because they were the "Ice puzzles of Reason." In his eyes they were first-rate and of the greatest importance: this was because of the grain of glass still in his eye. He made many patterns forming words, but he never could find out the right way to place them for one particular word, a word he was most anxious to make. It was "Eternity." The Snow Queen had said to him that if he could find out this word he should be his own master, and she would give him the whole world and a new pair of skates. But he could not discover it.

"Now I am going to fly away to the warm countries," said the Snow Queen. "I want to go and peep into the black cauldrons!" She meant the volcanoes Etna and Vesuvius by this. "I must whiten them a little; it does them good, and the lemons and the grapes too!" And away she flew.

Kay sat quite alone in all those many miles of empty ice halls. He looked at his bits of ice, and thought and thought, till something gave way within him. He sat so stiff and immovable that one might have thought he was frozen to death.

Then it was that little Gerda walked into the Palace, through the great gates in a biting wind. She said her evening prayer, and the wind dropped as if lulled to sleep, and she walked on into the big empty hall. She saw Kay, and knew him at once; she flung her arms round his neck, held him fast, and cried, "Kay, little Kay, have I found you at last?"

But he sat still, rigid and cold.

Then little Gerda shed hot tears; they fell upon his breast and penetrated to his heart. Here they thawed the lump of ice, and melted the little bit of the mirror which was in it. He looked at her, and she sang,—

> "Where roses deck the flowery vale,
> There, Infant Jesus, thee we hail!"

Then Kay burst into tears; he cried so much that the grain of glass was washed out of his eye. He knew her, and shouted with joy, "Gerda, dear little Gerda! where have you been for such a long time? And where have I been?" He looked round and said, "How cold it is here; how empty and vast!" He kept tight hold of Gerda, who laughed and cried for joy. Their happiness was so heavenly that even the bits of ice danced for joy around them; and when they settled down, there they lay! just in the very position the Snow Queen had told Kay he must find out, if he was to become his own master and have the whole world and a new pair of skates.

Gerda kissed his cheeks and they grew rosy, she kissed his eyes and they shone like hers, she kissed his hands and his feet, and he became well and strong. The Snow Queen might come home whenever she liked, his order of release was written there in shining letters of ice.

They took hold of each other's hands and wandered out of the big Palace. They talked about grandmother, and about the roses upon the roof. Wherever they went the winds lay still and the sun broke through the clouds. When they reached the bush with the red berries they found the reindeer waiting for them, and he had brought another young reindeer with him, whose udders were full. The children drank her warm

milk and kissed her on the mouth. Then they carried Kay and
Gerda, first to the Finn woman, in whose heated hut they
warmed themselves and received directions about the home-
ward journey. Then they went on to the Lapp woman; she
had made new clothes for them and prepared her sledge. Both
the reindeer ran by their side, to the boundaries of the
country; here the first green buds appeared, and they said
"Good-bye" to the reindeer and the Lapp woman. They heard
the first little birds twittering and saw the buds in the forest.
Out of it came riding a young girl on a beautiful horse, which
Gerda knew, for it had drawn the golden chariot. She had a
scarlet cap on her head and pistols in her belt; it was the
little robber girl, who was tired of being at home. She was
riding northwards to see how she liked it before she tried some
other part of the world. She knew them again, and Gerda
recognised her with delight.

"You are a nice fellow to go tramping off!" she said to
little Kay. "I should like to know if you deserve to have somebody running to the end of the world for your sake!"

But Gerda patted her cheek, and asked about the Prince
and Princess.

"They are travelling in foreign countries," said the robber
girl.

"But the crow?" asked Gerda.

"Oh, the crow is dead!" she answered. "The tame sweetheart is a widow, and goes about with a bit of black wool tied
round her leg. She pities herself bitterly, but it's all nonsense!
But tell me how you got on yourself, and where you found
him."

Gerda and Kay both told her all about it.

"Snip, snap, snurre, it's all right at last then!" she said, and she took hold of their hands and promised that if she ever passed through their town she would pay them a visit. Then she rode off into the wide world. But Kay and Gerda walked on, hand in hand, and wherever they went, they found the most delightful spring and blooming flowers. Soon they recognised the big town where they lived, with its tall towers, in which the bells still rang their merry peals. They went straight on to grandmother's door, up the stairs, and into her room. Everything was just as they had left it, and the old clock ticked in the corner, and the hands pointed to the time. As they went through the door into the room they perceived that they were grown up. The roses clustered round the open window, and there stood their two little chairs. Kay and Gerda sat down upon them, still holding each other by the hand. All the cold empty grandeur of the Snow Queen's palace had passed from their memory like a bad dream. Grandmother sat in God's warm sunshine reading from her Bible.

"Without ye become as little children ye cannot enter into the Kingdom of Heaven."

Kay and Gerda looked into each other's eyes, and then all at once the meaning of the old hymn came to them.

> "Where roses deck the flowery vale,
> There, Infant Jesus, we thee hail!"

And there they both sat, grown up and yet children, children at heart; and it was summer—warm, beautiful summer.

The Emperor's New Clothes

Many years ago there was an Emperor who was so exces-
sively fond of new clothes that he spent all his money on them.
He cared nothing about his soldiers nor for the theatre, nor
for driving in the woods except for the sake of showing off
his new clothes. He had a costume for every hour in the day,
and instead of saying as one does about any other King or
Emperor, "He is in his council chamber," here one always said,
"The Emperor is in his dressing-room."

Life was very gay in the great town where he lived; hosts
of strangers came to visit it every day, and among them one
day two swindlers. They gave themselves out as weavers, and
said that they knew how to weave the most beautiful stuffs
imaginable. Not only were the colours and patterns unusually
fine, but the clothes that were made of the stuffs had the
peculiar quality of becoming invisible to every person who was
not fit for the office he held, or if he was impossibly dull.

"Those must be splendid clothes," thought the Emperor.
"By wearing them I should be able to discover which men in
my kingdom are unfitted for their posts. I shall distinguish the
wise men from the fools. Yes, I certainly must order some of
that stuff to be woven for me."

He paid the two swindlers a lot of money in advance, so that
they might begin their work at once.

They did put up two looms and pretended to weave, but
they had nothing whatever upon their shuttles. At the outset

11*

they asked for a quantity of the finest silk and the purest gold thread, all of which they put into their own bags while they worked away at the empty looms far into the night.

"I should like to know how those weavers are getting on with the stuff," thought the Emperor; but he felt a little queer when he reflected that anyone who was stupid or unfit for his post would not be able to see it. He certainly thought that he need have no fears for himself, but still he thought he would send somebody else first to see how it was getting on. Everybody in the town knew what wonderful power the stuff possessed, and everyone was anxious to see how stupid his neighbour was.

"I will send my faithful old minister to the weavers," thought the Emperor. "He will be best able to see how the stuff looks, for he is a clever man and no one fulfils his duties better than he does!"

So the good old minister went into the room where the two swindlers sat working at the empty loom.

"Heaven preserve us!" thought the old minister, opening his eyes very wide. "Why I can't see a thing!" But he took care not to say so.

Both the swindlers begged him to be good enough to step a little nearer, and asked if he did not think it a good pattern and beautiful colouring. They pointed to the empty loom, and the poor old minister stared as hard as he could, but he could not see anything, for of course there was nothing to see.

"Good heavens!" thought he, "is it possible that I am a fool. I have never thought so, and nobody must know it. Am I not fit for my post? It will never do to say that I cannot see the stuffs."

"Well, sir, you don't say anything about the stuff," said

the one who was pretending to weave. "Oh, it is beautiful! quite charming!" said the old minister looking through his spectacles; "this pattern and these colours! I will certainly tell the Emperor that the stuff pleases me very much."

"We are delighted to hear you say so," said the swindlers, and then they named all the colours and described the peculiar pattern. The old minister paid great attention to what they said, so as to be able to repeat it when he got home to the Emperor.

Then the swindlers went on to demand more money, more silk, and more gold, to be able to proceed with the weaving; but they put it all into their own pockets—not a single strand was ever put into the loom, but they went on as before weaving at the empty loom.

The Emperor soon sent another faithful official to see how the stuff was getting on, and if it would soon be ready. The same thing happened to him as to the minister; he looked and looked, but as there was only the empty loom, he could see nothing at all.

"Is not this a beautiful piece of stuff?" said both the swindlers, showing and explaining the beautiful pattern and colours which were not there to be seen.

"I know I am not a fool!" thought the man "so it must be that I am unfit for my good post! It is very strange though! however one must not let it appear!" So he praised the stuff he did not see, and assured them of his delight in the beautiful colours and the originality of the design. "It is absolutely charming!" he said to the Emperor. Everybody in the town was talking about this splendid stuff.

Now the Emperor thought he would like to see it while it was still on the loom. So, accompanied by a number of selected courtiers, among whom were the two faithful officials who had already seen the imaginary stuff, he went to visit the crafty impostors, who were working away as hard as ever they could at the empty loom.

"It is magnificent!" said both the honest officials. "Only see, your Majesty, what a design! What colours!" And they pointed to the empty loom, for they thought no doubt the others could see the stuff.

"What!" thought the Emperor; "I see nothing at all! This is terrible! Am I a fool? Am I not fit to be Emperor? Why, nothing worse could happen to me!"

"Oh, it is beautiful!" said the Emperor. "It has my highest approval!" and he nodded his satisfaction as he gazed at the empty loom. Nothing would induce him to say that he could not see anything. The whole suite gazed and gazed, but saw nothing more than all the others. However, they all exclaimed with his Majesty, "It is very beautiful!" and they advised him to wear a suit made of this wonderful cloth on the occasion of a great procession which was just about to take place. "It is magnificent! gorgeous! excellent!" went from mouth to mouth; they were all equally delighted with it. The Emperor gave each of the rogues an order of knighthood to be worn in their buttonholes and the title of "Gentlemen weavers."

The swindlers sat up the whole night, before the day on which the procession was to take place, burning sixteen candles; so that people might see how anxious they were to get the Emperor's new clothes ready. They pretended to take the stuff off the loom. They cut it out in the air with a huge pair of scissors, and they stitched away with needles without any thread in them. At last they said: "Now the Emperor's new clothes are ready!"

The Emperor, with his grandest courtiers, went to them himself, and both the swindlers raised one arm in the air, as if they were holding something, and said: "See, these are the trousers, this is the coat, here is the mantle!" and so on. "It is as light as a spider's web. One might think one had nothing on, but that is the very beauty of it!"

"Yes!" said all the courtiers, but they could not see anything, for there was nothing to see.

"Will your imperial majesty be graciously pleased to take off your clothes," said the impostors, "so that we may put on the new ones, along here before the great mirror."

The Emperor took off all his clothes, and the impostors pretended to give him one article of dress after the other, of the new ones which they had pretended to make. They pretended to fasten something round his waist and to tie on something; this was the train, and the Emperor turned round and round in front of the mirror.

"How well his majesty looks in the new clothes! How becoming they are!" cried all the people round. "What a design, and what colours! They are most gorgeous robes!"

"The canopy is waiting outside which is to be carried over your majesty in the procession," said the master of the ceremonies.

"Well, I am quite ready," said the Emperor. "Don't the clothes fit well?" and then he turned round again in front of the mirror, so that he should seem to be looking at his grand things.

The chamberlains who were to carry the train stooped and pretended to lift it from the ground with both hands, and they walked along with their hands in the air. They dared not let it appear that they could not see anything.

Then the Emperor walked along in the procession under the gorgeous canopy, and everybody in the streets and at the windows exclaimed, "How beautiful the Emperor's new clothes are! What a splendid train! And they fit to perfection!"

Nobody would let it appear that he could see nothing, for then he would not be fit for his post, or else he was a fool.

None of the Emperor's clothes had been so successful before.

"But he has got nothing on," said a little child.

"Oh, listen to the innocent," said its father; and one person whispered to the other what the child had said. "He has nothing on; a child says he has nothing on!"

"But he has nothing on!" at last cried all the people.

The Emperor writhed, for he knew it was true, but he thought "the procession must go on now," so held himself stiffer than ever, and the chamberlains held up the invisible train.

The Swineherd

There was once a poor Prince; he had only quite a tiny kingdom, but it was big enough to allow him to marry, and he was bent upon marrying.

Now, it certainly was rather bold of him to say to the Emperor's daughter, "Will you have me?" He did, however, venture to say so, for his name was known far and wide; and there were hundreds of Princesses who would have said "Yes," and "Thank you, kindly," but see if *she* would!

Just let us hear about it.

A rose tree grew on the grave of the Prince's father, it was such a beautiful rose tree; it only bloomed every fifth year, and then only bore one blossom; but what a rose that was! By merely smelling it one forgot all one's cares and sorrows.

Then he had a nightingale which sang as if every lovely melody in the world dwelt in her little throat. This rose and this nightingale were to be given to the Princess, so they were put into great silver caskets and sent to her.

The Emperor had them carried before him into the great Hall where the Princess was playing at "visiting" with her ladies-in-waiting; they had nothing else to do. When she saw the caskets with the gifts she clapped her hands with delight!

"If only it were a little pussy cat!" said she—but there was the lovely rose.

"Oh, how exquisitely it is made!" said all the ladies-in-waiting.

"It is more than beautiful," said the Emperor; "it is neat." But the Princess touched it, and then she was ready to cry. "Fie, papa!" she said; "it is not made, it is a real one!"

"Fie," said all the ladies-in-waiting; "it is a real one!"

"Well, let us see what there is in the other casket, before we get angry," said the Emperor, and out came the nightingale. It sang so beautifully that at first no one could find anything to say against it.

"*Superbe! charmant!*" said the ladies-in-waiting, for they all had a smattering of French, one spoke it worse than the other.

"How that bird reminds me of our lamented Empress's musical box," said an old courtier. "Ah, yes, they are the same tunes, and the same beautiful execution."

"So they are," said the Emperor, and he cried like a little child.

"I should hardly think it could be a real one," said the Princess.

"Yes, it is a real one," said those who had brought it.

"Oh, let that bird fly away then," said the Princess, and she would not hear of allowing the Prince to come. But he was not to be crushed; he stained his face brown and black, and, pressing his cap over his eyes, he knocked at the door.

"Good-morning, Emperor," said he; "can I be taken into service in the palace?"

"Well, there are so many wishing to do that," said the Emperor; "but let me see!—yes, I need somebody to look after the pigs, for we have so many of them."

So the Prince was made imperial swineherd. A horrid little room was given him near the pig-sties, and here he had to live. He sat busily at work all day, and by the evening he had made

a beautiful little cooking pot; it had bells all round it, and
when the pot boiled they tinkled delightfully and played the
old tune:

> "Ach du lieber Augustin,
> Alles ist weg, weg, weg!"[1]

But the greatest charm of all about it was, that by holding
one's finger in the steam one could immediately smell all the
dinners that were being cooked at every stove in the town.
Now this was a very different matter from a rose.

The Princess came walking along with all her ladies-in-
waiting, and when she heard the tune she stopped and
looked pleased, for she could play "Ach du lieber Augustin"
herself; it was her only tune, and she could only play it with
one finger.

"Why, that is my tune," she said; "this must be a cultivated
swineherd. Go and ask him what the instrument costs."

So one of the ladies-in-waiting had to go into his room,
but she put pattens on first.

"How much do you want for the pot," she asked.

"I must have ten kisses from the Princess," said the swineherd.

"Heaven preserve us!" said the lady.

"I won't take less," said the swineherd.

"Well what does he say?" asked the Princess.

"I really cannot tell you," said the lady-in-waiting, "it is so
shocking."

"Then you must whisper it." And she whispered it.

"He is a wretch!" said the Princess, and went away at once.

> [1]Alas! dear Augustin,
> All is lost, lost, lost!

But she had only gone a little way when she heard the bells tinkling beautifully:

"Ach du lieber Augustin."

"Go and ask him if he will take ten kisses from the ladies-in-waiting."

"No, thank you," said the swineherd; "ten kisses from the Princess, or I keep my pot."

"How tiresome it is," said the Princess. "Then you will have to stand round me, so that no one may see."

So the ladies-in-waiting stood round her and spread out their skirts while the swineherd took his ten kisses, and then the pot was hers.

What a delight it was to them. The pot was kept on the boil day and night. They knew what was cooking on every stove in the town, from the chamberlain's to the shoemaker's. The ladies-in-waiting danced about and clapped their hands.

"We know who has sweet soup and pancakes for dinner, and who has cutlets; how amusing it is."

"Highly interesting," said the mistress of the robes.

"Yes, but hold your tongues, for I am the Emperor's daughter."

"Heaven preserve us!" they all said.

The swineherd—that is to say, the Prince, only nobody knew that he was not a real swineherd—did not let the day pass in idleness, and he now constructed a rattle. When it was swung round it played all the waltzes, galops and jig tunes which have ever been heard since the creation of the world.

"But this is *superbe!*" said the Princess, as she walked by. "I have never heard finer compositions. Go and ask him what the instrument costs, but let us have no more kissing."

"He wants a hundred kisses from the Princess!" said the lady-in-waiting.

"I think he is mad!" said the Princess, and she went away, but she had not gone far when she stopped.

"One must encourage art," she said; "I am the Emperor's daughter. Tell him he can have ten kisses, the same as yesterday, and he can take the others from the ladies-in-waiting."

"But we don't like that at all" said the ladies.

"Oh, nonsense! If I can kiss him you can do the same. Remember that I pay your wages as well as give you board and lodging." So the lady-in-waiting had to go again.

"A hundred kisses from the Princess, or let each keep his own."

"Stand in front of me," said she, and all the ladies stood round, while he kissed her.

"Whatever is the meaning of that crowd round the pigsties?" said the Emperor as he stepped out on to the verandah; he rubbed his eyes and put on his spectacles. "Why, it is the ladies-in-waiting, what game are they up to? I must go and see!" so he pulled up the heels of his slippers for they were shoes which he had trodden down.

Bless us, what a hurry he was in! When he got into the yard, he walked very softly and the ladies were so busy counting the kisses, so that there should be fair play, and neither too few nor too many kisses, that they never heard the Emperor. He stood on tiptoe.

"What is all this?" he said when he saw what was going on, and he hit them on the head with his slipper just as the swineherd was taking the eighty-sixth kiss.

"Out you go!" said the Emperor, for he was furious, and both the Princess and the Prince were put out of his realm.

There she stood crying, and the swineherd scolded, and the rain poured down in torrents.

"Oh, miserable creature that I am! if only I had accepted the handsome Prince. Oh, how unhappy I am!"

The swineherd went behind a tree, wiped the black and brown stain from his face, and threw away his ugly clothes. Then he stepped out dressed as a Prince, he was so handsome that the Princess could not help curtseying to him.

"I am come to despise thee," he said. "Thou wouldst not have an honourable prince, thou couldst not prize the rose or the nightingale, but thou wouldst kiss the swineherd for a trumpery musical box! As thou hast made thy bed, so must thou lie upon it!"

Then he went back into his own little kingdom and shut and locked the door. So she had to stand outside and sing in earnest—

> "Ach du lieber Augustin,
> Alles ist weg, weg, weg!"

The Bell

In the evening, at sunset, when glimpses of golden clouds could just be seen among the chimney pots, a curious sound would be heard, first by one person, then by another; it was like a church bell, but it only lasted a moment because of the rumble of vehicles and the street cries.

"There is the evening bell," people would say; "the sun is setting."

Those who went outside the town where the houses were more scattered, each with its garden or little meadow, saw the evening star, and heard the tones of the bell much better. It seemed as if the sound came from a church buried in silent, fragrant woods, and people looked in that direction, feeling quite solemn.

Time passed, and still people said one to the other, "Can there be a church in the woods! that bell has such a wonderfully sweet sound; shall we go and look at it closer." The rich people drove and the poor ones walked, but it was a very long way; when they reached a group of willows which grew on the outskirts of the wood, they sat down and looked up among the long branches, thinking that they were really in the heart of the forest. A confectioner from the town came out and pitched a tent there, and then another confectioner, and he hung a bell up over his tent. This bell was tarred so as to stand the rain, and the clapper was wanting. When people went home again they said it had been so romantic, and that meant something beyond mere tea. Three persons protested that they had penetrated right through the forest to the other side, and that they had heard the same curious bell all the time, but that then it sounded as if it came from the town.

One of them wrote a poem about it, and said that it sounded like a mother's voice to a beloved child, no melody could be sweeter than the chimes of this bell.

The Emperor's attention was also drawn to it, and he promised that anyone who really discovered where the sound came from should receive the title of "the world's bell-ringer," even if there were no bell at all.

A great many people went to the woods for the sake of earning an honest penny, but only one of them brought home any kind of explanation. No one had been far enough, not even he himself, but he said that the sound of the bell came from a very big owl in a hollow tree; it was a wise owl, which perpetually beat its head against a tree, but whether the sound came from its head or from the hollow tree he could not say with any certainty. All the same he was appointed "world's bell-ringer," and every year he wrote a little treatise on the owl, but nobody was much the wiser for it.

Now on a certain Confirmation day the priest had preached a very moving sermon, all the young people about to be confirmed had been much touched by it; it was a very important day for them. They were leaving childhood behind and becoming grown-up persons, the child's soul was, as it were, to be transformed into that of a responsible being. It was a beautiful sunny day, and after the Confirmation the young people walked out of the town and they heard the sound of the unknown bell more than usually loud coming from the wood. On hearing it they all felt anxious to go further and see it; all except three. The first of these had to go home to try on her ball-dress; it was this very dress and this very ball which were the reason of her having been confirmed this time; otherwise it would have been put off. The second was a poor boy, who had borrowed his tail-coat and boots of the landlord's son, and he had to return them at the appointed time. The third said that he had never been anywhere without his parents, that he had always been a good child and he meant to continue so, although he was confirmed; nobody ought to have made fun of this resolve, but he did not escape being laughed at.

So these three did not go; the others trudged off. The sun shone and the birds sang, and the newly-confirmed young people took each other by the hand and sang with them; they had not yet received any position in life, they were all equal in the eye of the Lord on the day of their Confirmation. Soon two of the smallest ones got tired and they returned to town; two little girls sat down and made wreaths, so they did not go either. When the others reached the willows where the confectioners had their tents, they said, "Now, then, here we are; the bell doesn't exist, it is only something people imagine!"

Just then the bell was heard in the wood, with its deep rich notes; and four or five of them decided after all to penetrate further into the wood. The underwood was so thick and close that it was quite difficult to advance. The woodruff grew almost too high, convolvulus and brambles hung in long garlands from tree to tree, where the nightingales sang and the sunbeams played. It was deliciously peaceful, but there was no path for the girls, their clothes would have been torn to shreds. There were great boulders over-grown with many-coloured mosses, and fresh springs trickled among them with a curious little gurgling sound.

"Surely that cannot be the bell!" said one of the young people, as he lay down to listen.

"This must be thoroughly looked into." So he stayed behind and let the others go on.

They came to a little hut made of bark, and branches overhung by a crab-apple, as if it wanted to shake all its bloom over the roof, which was covered with roses. The long sprays clustered round the gable, and on it hung a little bell. Could this be the one they sought? Yes, they were all agreed that it must be, except one; he said it was far too small and delicate to be heard so far away as they had heard it, and that the tones which moved all hearts were quite different from these. He who spoke was a king's son, and so the others said: "That kind of fellow must always be wiser than anyone else."

So they let him go on alone, and as he went he was more and more overcome by the solitude of the wood; but he still heard the little bell with which the others were so pleased, and now and then when the wind came from the direction of the confectioners he could hear demands for tea.

But the deep-toned bell sounded above them all, and it seemed as if there was an organ playing with it, and the sounds came from the left, where the heart is placed.

There was a rustling among the bushes, and a little boy stood before the king's son; he had wooden shoes on, and such a small jacket that the sleeves did not cover his wrists. They knew each other, for he was the boy who had had to go back to return the coat and the boots to the landlord's son. He had done this, changed back into his shabby clothes and wooden shoes, and then, drawn by the deep notes of the bell, had returned to the wood again. "Then we can go together," said the king's son. But the poor boy in the wooden shoes was too bashful. He pulled down his short sleeves, and said he was afraid he could not walk quickly enough, besides which he thought the bell ought to be looked for on the right, because that side looked the most beautiful.

"Then we shan't meet at all," said the king's son, nodding to the poor boy, who went into the thickest and darkest part of the wood, where the thorns tore his shabby clothes and scratched his face, hands, and feet till they bled. The king's son got some good scratches too, but he at least had the sun shining upon his path. We are going to follow him, for he is a bright fellow.

"I must and will find the bell," said he, "if I have to go to the end of the world."

Some horrid monkeys sat up in the trees grinning and showing their teeth.

"Shall we pelt him?" said they. "Shall we thrash him; he is a king's son."

But he went confidently on further and further into the wood, where the most extraordinary flowers grew. There were white star-like lilies with blood-red stamens, pale blue tulips which glistened in the sun, and apple trees on which the apples looked like great shining soap-bubbles. You may fancy how these trees glittered in the sun. Round about were beautiful green meadows, where stags and hinds gambolled under the spreading oaks and beeches. Mosses and creepers grew in the fissures where the bark of the trees was broken away. There were also great glades with quiet lakes, where white swans swam about flapping their wings. The king's son often stopped and listened, for he sometimes fancied that the bell sounded from one of these lakes; but then again he felt sure that it was not there, but further in the wood.

Now the sun began to go down, and the clouds were fiery red; a great stillness came over the wood, and he sank upon his knees, sang his evening psalm, and said, "Never shall I find what I seek, now the sun is going down, the night is coming on—the dark night; perhaps I could catch one more glimpse of the round, red sun before it sinks beneath the earth. I will climb up on to those rocks; they are as high as the trees."

He seized the roots and creepers, and climbed up the slippery stones where the water-snakes wriggled and the toads seemed to croak at him; but he reached the top before the sun disappeared. Seen from this height, oh! what splendour lay before him! The ocean, the wide, beautiful ocean, its long waves rolling towards the shore. The sun still stood like a great shining altar, out there where sea and sky met. Everything melted away into glowing colours; the wood sang, the ocean sang, and his heart sang with them. All Nature was like a vast holy temple, where trees and floating clouds were as pillars, flowers and grass the woven tapestry, and the heaven itself a great dome. The red colours vanished as the sun went down, but millions of stars peeped out; they were like countless diamond lamps, and the king's son spread out his arms towards heaven, sea, and forest. At that moment, from the right-hand path came the poor boy with the short sleeves and wooden shoes. He had reached the same goal just as soon by his own road. They ran towards each other, and clasped each other's hands in that great temple of Nature and Poetry, and above them sounded the invisible holy bell; happy spirits floated round it to the strains of a joyous Hallelujah.

Olé Luköié, the Dustman

There is nobody in all the world who can tell so many stories as Olé Luköié! And such stories as he can tell!

When night is drawing on, and the children are sitting round the table as good as possible, or on their little foot-stools, in walks Old Shut-eyes. He comes so quietly up the stairs without his shoes, and opens the door so softly that nobody hears him; and puff! he sends a shower of milk into their eyes in such fine spray as to be invisible; but they can't keep their eyes open after it, and so they never see him. He steals behind them and breathes upon their necks, making their heads as heavy as lead; but he never hurts them; he does it all from kindness to the children. He only wants them to be quiet, and the best way to make them quiet is to have them in bed; when they are settled there, he can tell them his stories.

Then as soon as the children are asleep, Olé Luköié seats himself upon their beds. He is well dressed; his clothes are all of silk but it is impossible to say what colour they are, for it shimmers green, red, and blue every time he turns. He has an umbrella under his arm, one with pictures on it, and this he holds over the good children, and then they dream the most delightful stories all night long. The other umbrella has no pictures on it, and he holds this one over the children who have been naughty, and then they sleep heavily till the morning and have no dreams at all.

I am now going to tell you about a little boy to whom Olé Luköié went every night for a whole week. His name was Hialmar. There are just seven stories, because there are seven days in a week.

Monday

"Now, just listen!" said Olé Luköié, in the evening, when he had got Hialmar to bed. "First I will smarten things up a bit," and then all the plants in pots became big trees, with their branches stretching right up to the ceiling and along the walls, so that the room looked like a delightful arbour. The branches were covered with flowers, and the flowers were more beautiful than roses; they had the most delightful scent, and, if you tried to eat them, were more delicious than the very nicest jam. The fruit shone like gold, and then there were buns bursting with plums; they were splendid!

All at once the most miserable grumbles came from the table-drawer where Hialmar's schoolbooks were kept.

"What is that now?" said Olé Luköié, going along and opening the drawer.

It was the slate groaning and writhing because there was a wrong figure in the sum set on it, and it was ready to fall to pieces.

The pencil was hopping and skipping at the end of its piece of string, just as if it had been a little dog which would like to try and do the sum, but it couldn't! Then there was Hialmar's copybook clamouring away inside its covers most pitifully. There was a row of capital letters down each side on every leaf, each with a little one beside it; then beside them letters which imagined that they looked like them, but these were written by Hialmar. They looked almost as if they had tumbled over the line on which they ought to have been standing upright.

"See, this is how you ought to hold yourselves!" said the headlines, "so—to one side with a brisk flourish!"

"Oh, we should like nothing better," said Hialmar's letters, "but we can't, we are so crooked!"

"Then you shall have a dose of medicine," said Olé Luköié.

"Oh, no!" they cried, and then they stood up as stiffly as possible.

"Well, now we can't tell any stories!" said Olé Luköié. "I must drill them! One, two! One, two!" and then he drilled the letters and they stood up stiffer than any headlines could stand. But when Olé Luköié went away and Hialmar woke up in the morning they were as crooked as ever.

Tuesday

As soon as Hialmar was in bed, Olé Luköié touched all the furniture in the room with his little wooden wand, and everything began to talk. They all talked about themselves except the spittoon, which was silent and much annoyed that they were all so vain as only to talk about themselves, and to pay no attention to him, standing so modestly in the corner and allowing himself to be spat upon. There was a big picture in a gilt frame hanging over the chest of drawers; it was a landscape in which one saw tall, old trees, flowers growing in the grass, and a great piece of water, with a river flowing from it round behind a wood, past many castles and away to the open sea.

Olé Luköié touched the picture with his wand, and the birds in it began to sing, the branches of the trees moved, and the clouds scudded along; you could see their shadows passing over the landscape.

Now Olé Luköié lifted little Hialmar up close to the frame, and Hialmar put his leg right into the picture among the long grass, and there he stood; the sun shone down upon him through the branches of the trees. He ran to the water and got into a little boat which lay there, it was painted red and white, and the sails shone like silver. Six swans, all with golden crowns round their necks, and a shining blue star upon their heads, drew the boat past the dark green woods, where the trees told stories about robbers and witches; and the flowers told other stories about the pretty little elves, and all that the butterflies had told them.

Beautiful fish with gold and silver scales swam after the boat; every now and then they sprang out of the water and back again with a splash. Red and blue birds, large and small, flew in two long lines behind them; the gnats buzzed, and the cockchafers boomed; they all wanted to go with Hialmar, and each of them had a story to tell.

That was a sailing trip indeed! Now the woods were thick and dark, now they were like beautiful gardens full of sunshine and flowers, and among them were castles of glass and marble. Princesses stood upon the balconies, and they were all little girls whom Hialmar knew and used to play with.

They stretched out their hands, each one holding the most beautiful sugar pig which any cakewoman could sell. Hialmar took hold of one end of the pig as they sailed by, and the princess held the other tight, and each had a share, she the smaller and Hialmar the bigger! Little princes stood sentry by each castle; they saluted with golden swords, and showered down sugar plums and tin soldiers; they were princes indeed.

Now he sailed through a wood, now through great halls, or right through a town; he passed through the one where his nurse lived, she who used to carry him about when he was quite a little boy and who was so fond of him. She nodded and waved her hand to him, and sang a pretty little song which she had written herself and sent to Hialmar:

"I dream of thee for many an hour.
Hialmar, my own, my sweeting;
My kisses once fell like a shower,
Thy brow and red cheeks greeting.

"Mine ear thy first formed word addressed,
Thy last must be in parting;
May you on earth by Heaven be blessed,
Angel, from Heavenward darting!"

All the birds sang too, the flowers danced upon their stalks, and the old trees nodded, just as if Olé Luköié were telling them stories.

Wednesday

How the rain was pouring down outside! Hialmar could even hear it in his sleep, and when Olé Luköié opened the window, the water stood right up to the sill; it was a regular lake, and a beautiful ship lay close up to the house.

"Will you sail with me, little Hialmar?" said Olé Luköié; "if you will, you can go to distant countries to-night, and be back here again in the morning!"

Then all at once Hialmar found himself in his best Sunday clothes on board the beautiful ship; it was heavenly weather, and they sailed through the streets, past the church, till they reached a wild open sea. They sailed so far that there was no more land to be seen. They saw a flock of storks leaving home on their way to the warm countries, flying in a line, one behind the other; they had already flown a long, long way. One of them was so tired that his wings could hardly carry him any further; he was the last one in the row, and soon he was a long way behind. At last he sank, with outspread wings, lower and lower; he flapped his wings feebly for a few strokes, but it was no use. Now he touched the rigging of the ship with his feet, and slid down the sail with a flop on to the deck.

Then the cabin boy picked him up and put him into the henhouse, with the chickens, and ducks and turkeys; the poor stork stood among them looking quite depressed.

"What a creature!" said all the hens. The turkey-cock puffed himself up as big as he could, and asked who he was;

and the ducks waddled backwards, pushing against each other, saying, "Quack, quack!"

Then the stork told them about sunny Africa, and the pyramids, and the ostrich running across the deserts like a wild horse; but the ducks did not understand him, and they pushed each other and said, "Are we agreed that he is an idiot?"

"Yes, indeed, he's an idiot," said the turkey-cock with a gobble. Then the stork became quite silent, and thought about his beloved Africa.

"Nice thin legs you've got!" said the turkey-cock; "how much a yard?"

"Quack, quack, quack!" grinned all the ducks, but the stork appeared not to hear them.

"You're quite at liberty to laugh too," said the turkey-cock to him; "it was a very witty remark, or perhaps it was too low for you, gobble, gobble. He's not many-sided," he said to the others; "it's good enough to amuse us!" Then all the hens clucked and the ducks quacked; it was tremendous the amusement they got out of it.

But Hialmar went along to the henhouse, opened the door, and called the stork, and it hopped out on to the deck to him. It was rested now, and it seemed to nod to Hialmar to thank him; thereupon it spread its wings and flew away to the warm countries. But the hens clucked, the ducks quacked, and the turkey-cock's head got as red as fire.

"To-morrow we'll make you into soup," said Hialmar, and then he woke up and found himself lying in his own little bed. That was an extraordinary journey Olé Luköié had taken him.

Thursday

"I'll tell you what!" said Olé Luköié; "don't be frightened, and I will show you a little mouse." And he stretched out his hand with the tiny little animal in it. "It has come to invite you to a wedding. There are two little mice who intend to enter the wedded state to-night. They live under the floor of your mother's larder, which they say is a most delightful residence."

"But how can I get through a little mouse-hole in the floor?" said Hialmar.

"Leave that to me," said Olé Luköié; "I'll soon make you small enough!"

Then he touched Hialmar with his wand, and he quickly grew smaller and smaller; at last he was not as tall as one's finger.

"Now you may borrow the tin soldier's clothes; I think they'll just fit you, and it looks so smart to have on a uniform when one's in company."

"Yes indeed!" said Hialmar, and in a moment he was dressed like the grandest tin soldier.

"Be so good as to take a seat in your mother's thimble," said the little mouse, "and I shall have the honour of drawing you!"

"Heavens! are you going to take that trouble yourself, young lady?" said Hialmar, and off they drove to the mouse's wedding.

First they went down under the floor into a long passage, which was just high enough for them to drive through, and the whole passage was lighted up with touch-wood.

"Isn't there a delicious smell here?" said the mouse who was drawing him; "the whole passage has been smeared over with bacon fat! Nothing could be nicer."

Then they came to the bridal hall, where all the little lady mice stood on the right whispering and giggling, as if they were making fun of each other, and on the left stood all the gentlemen mice stroking their whiskers with their paws. The bridal pair stood in the middle of the room, in the hollow rind of a cheese, kissing each other most energetically before all the other people, but then they were engaged, you know, and just about to be married.

More and more visitors poured in, the mice were almost crushing each other to death, and the bridal pair had taken their place in the doorway, so that one could neither get in nor out. The whole room, like the passage, was smeared with bacon fat; there were no other refreshments, but for dessert a pea was produced, in which one of the little mice of the family had bitten the name of the bridal pair; that is to say the first letter of it, and this was something quite extraordinary.

All the mice said it was a delightful wedding and the conversation most entertaining.

And then Hialmar drove home again; he had been in very grand company, but in order to get there he had been obliged to shrink wonderfully, to make himself small enough to get into the uniform of a tin soldier.

Friday

"It is astounding what a number of grown-up people would like to get hold of me!" said Olé Luköié, "especially those with a bad conscience. 'Good little Olé,' they say to me, 'we can't close our eyes, and there we lie all night with all our bad deeds staring us in the face. They are like naughty elfins; they come and sit on our beds and squirt hot water over us. Won't you come and chase them away so that we may have a good sleep?' and then they sigh deeply. 'We will gladly pay you, Olé; good-night. You will find the money on the window-sill.' But I don't do it for money!" said Olé Luköié.

"What are we going to do to-night?" asked Hialmar.

"Well, I don't know whether you would like to go to a wedding again to-night; it's a different kind from yesterday's. Your sister's big doll, the one which looks like a man, and is called Herman, is to be married to Bertha; besides which, it is her birthday, so there will be no end of presents."

"Oh, I know all about that; whenever the dolls want new clothes my sister lets them have a birthday or a wedding. It has happened hundreds of times!"

"Yes, but to-night it's the hundred and first wedding, and the hundred and first is the end of all things, so that's why this one will be so grand. Just look!"

Hialmar looked along at the table; there was the little pasteboard house with lights in the windows, and all the tin soldiers presenting arms outside. The bridal pair sat upon the floor leaning against the leg of the table; they were very thoughtful, and they had reason to be. Olé Luköié, dressed in grandmother's black skirt, married them; when the ceremony was over, all the furniture in the room joined in singing the following pretty song which had been written by the pencil; it went to the tune of the tattoo.

> "Our song shall swing like the wind, like the wind.
> Till the bridal pair are enshrin'd, are enshrin'd,
> And they curtsey both like a stick, do you mind?
> For they're wood inside with kid for a rind.
> Hurrah! hurrah! wood and skin well combin'd,
> We'll sing it aloud to the rain and the wind!"

Then the presents were given, but they had declined any eatables: love was enough for them without anything else.

"Shall we go into the country or travel abroad?" asked the bridegroom, and then they consulted the swallow which had travelled so much, and the old mother hen which had reared five broods of chickens. The swallow told them all about the delightful warm countries where the grapes hung in luscious clusters, and where the air was so mild, and the colours on the mountains were such as were not to be found elsewhere.

"But they haven't got our green cabbage," said the hen. "I was in the country all one summer with my chicks; there was a gravel pit that we scratched in all day, and then we got admission to a garden where the cabbage grew! Oh, how green it was! I can't imagine anything more beautiful."

"But one cabbage is just like another," said the swallow, "and then there's so much bad weather here!"

"Oh, we're used to that," said the hen.

"But it's so cold, it freezes."

"That's good for the cabbage," said the hen. "Besides, sometimes it is warm enough. Four years ago didn't we have a summer with tremendous heat, for five weeks one could hardly breathe! And then we don't have all the poisonous creatures they have abroad, and there are no robbers. Anyone who doesn't think our own country the best, must be a fool! He doesn't deserve to live here." And the hen began to cry. "I've had my journeys too; I once travelled twelve miles in a barrel, and there's no pleasure in travelling."

"Ah, the hen is a wise woman!" said Bertha the doll. "I don't like travelling among mountains either, for first you go up and then you go down! No, we will move out by the gravel pit and take our walks in the cabbage garden."

And that was the end of it.

Saturday

"Are we going to have some stories?" asked little Hialmar, as soon as Olé Luköié had got him to bed.

"We haven't time for any to-night," said Olé, as he opened his prettiest umbrella. "Just look at these Chinese!" The whole umbrella looked exactly like a big Chinese bowl, with blue trees all over it, and arched bridges on which stood little people nodding their heads. "We must have the whole world polished up for tomorrow," said Olé; "it is a holiday, for it is Sunday. I must go up into the church tower to see if the little church brownies are polishing the bells so that they may sound well. I must go into the fields to see if the wind has blown the dust off the grass and leaves. My biggest piece of work is to get down all the stars to polish them; I take them in my apron; but first I have to number each one, and the holes they belong to have to be numbered too, so that they may go back into their proper places, or they wouldn't stick, and then we should be having too many falling stars, one after the other would drop out."

"Now I say, Mr. Luköié," said one of the old portraits hanging on the wall, "I am Hialmar's great-grandfather; I am much obliged to you for telling him stories, but you mustn't puzzle his brains. The stars can't be taken down to be polished! The stars are planets just like our own earth, and that's the best of them!"

"Much obliged to you, old great-grandfather," said Olé

Luköié. "My best thanks to you; you are the head of the family; you are an antiquity, but I am older than you! I am an old heathen; the Greeks and Romans call me the Dream-god! I have my footing in the grandest houses; I can get on both with big and little! You may tell the stories yourself!" And then Olé Luköié went away and took his umbrella with him.

"I suppose one mayn't give an opinion now!" said the old portrait.

And then Hialmar woke.

Sunday

"Good-evening," said Olé Luköié, and Hialmar nodded; and then he jumped up and turned great-grandfather's portrait with its face to the wall, so that it should not talk as it did last time.

"Now you must tell me some stories about 'The five green peas which lived in a peaspod,' and about the 'Cock paying his addresses to the hen,' and about the 'Darning-needle' which was so fine that it fancied it was an ordinary needle!"

"You may have too much of a good thing," said Olé Luköié; "I would rather show you something you know! I will show you my brother; he is also called Olé Luköié, but he never comes more than once to anybody, and when he comes he takes them away with him on his horse, and tells them stories. He only knows two, one which is so beautiful that nobody on earth can imagine it, and one which is too horrible to be described!" And then Olé lifted little Hialmar up to the window, and said, "Now you can see my brother, the other Olé Luköié! He is also called Death; you see he doesn't look at all bad, as he sometimes does in pictures, all bones and joints! No, he has a silver embroidered border round his coat; it is a Hussar's uniform, and a black velvet cloak streams out behind over his horse's back! See how they are galloping."

And Hialmar saw how Olé Luköié rode off, taking both old and young with him on his horse. He put some of them before him and some behind, but he always asked first, "What character have you in your mark book?" They all said "good." "Let me see myself," said he, and then they had to show him the book. All those who had "very good" or "excellent" against their names were put up in front of him, and were told the most delightful stories; but those who had only "pretty good" or "tolerable," had to sit behind him, and were told horrible stories. They shivered, and cried, and tried to get off the horse, but they couldn't do that, because they grew fast to it at once.

"But Death is a beautiful Olé Luköié," said Hialmar. "I am not a bit afraid of him!"

"Nor need you be," said Olé Luköié; "if only you take care to have a good character in your book."

"Ah, now, that's instructive!" mumbled great-grandfather's portrait. "It's some good after all to speak one's mind!" and he was quite pleased.

Now this is the story about Olé Luköié! To-night he can tell you some more himself.

The Tinder Box

A soldier came marching along the high road. One, two! One, two! He had his knapsack on his back and his sword at his side, for he had been to the wars, and he was on his way home now. He met an old witch on the road, she was so ugly, her lower lip hung right down on to her chin.

She said, "Good-evening, soldier! What a nice sword you've got, and such a big knapsack; you are a real soldier! You shall have as much money as ever you like!"

"Thank you kindly, you old witch!" said the soldier.

"Do you see that big tree!" said the witch, pointing to a tree close by. "It is hollow inside! Climb up to the top and you will see a hole into which you can let yourself down, right down under the tree! I will tie a rope round your waist so that I can haul you up again when you call!"

"What am I to do down under the tree?" asked the soldier.

"Fetch money!" said the witch. "You must know that when you get down to the bottom of the tree you will find yourself in a wide passage; it's quite light there, for there are over a hundred blazing lamps. You will see three doors which you can open, for the keys are there. If you go into the first room you will see a big box in the middle of the floor. A dog is sitting on the top of it, and he has eyes as big as saucers, but you needn't mind that. I will give you my blue-checked apron, which you can spread out on the floor; then go quickly forward, take up the dog and put him on my

apron, open the box and take out as much money as ever
you like. It is all copper, but if you like silver better, go into
the next room. There you will find a dog with eyes as big as
millstones: but never mind that, put him on my apron and
take the money. If you prefer gold you can have it too, and
as much as you can carry, if you go into the third room. But
the dog sitting on that box has eyes each as big as the Round
Tower. He *is* a dog, indeed, as you may imagine! But don't
let it trouble you; you only have to put him on to my apron
and then he won't hurt you, and you can take as much gold
out of the box as you like!"

"That's not so bad!" said the soldier. "But what am I to
give you, old witch? For you'll want something, I'll be
bound."

"No," said the witch, "not a single penny do I want;
I only want you to bring me an old tinder box that my grandmother forgot the last time she was down there!"

"Well! tie the rope round my waist!" said the soldier.

"Here it is," said the witch, "and here is my blue-checked
apron."

Then the soldier climbed up the tree, let himself slide down
the hollow trunk, and found himself, as the witch had said, in
the wide passage where the many hundred lamps were burning.

Now he opened the first door. Ugh! There sat the dog
with eyes as big as saucers staring at him.

"You are a nice fellow!" said the soldier, as he put him on
to the witch's apron, and took out as many pennies as he
could cram into his pockets. Then he shut the box, and put
the dog on the top of it again, and went into the next room.
Hallo! there sat the dog with eyes as big as millstones.

"You shouldn't stare at me so hard; you might get a pain in your eyes!" Then he put the dog on the apron, but when he saw all the silver in the box he threw away all the coppers, and stuffed his pockets and his knapsack with silver. Then he went into the third room. Oh! how horrible! that dog really had two eyes as big as the Round Tower, and they rolled round and round like wheels.

"Good-evening!" said the soldier, saluting, for he had never seen such a dog in his life; but after looking at him for a bit he thought, "that will do," and then he lifted him down on to the apron and opened the chest. Preserve us! What a lot of gold! He could buy the whole of Copenhagen with it, and all the sugar pigs from the cake-woman, all the tin soldiers, whips, and rocking-horses in the world! That was money indeed! Now the soldier threw away all the silver he had filled his pockets and his knapsack with, and put gold in its place. Yes, he crammed all his pockets, his knapsack, his cap, and his boots so full that he could hardly walk! Now, he really had got a lot of money. He put the dog back on to the box, shut the door, and shouted up through the tree, "Haul me up, you old witch!"

"Have you got the tinder box?"

"Oh! to be sure!" said the soldier. "I had quite forgotten it." And he went back to fetch it. The witch hauled him up, and there he was standing on the high road again with his pockets, boots, knapsack, and cap full of gold.

"What do you want the tinder box for?" asked the soldier.

"That's no business of yours," said the witch. "You've got the money; give me the tinder box!"

"Rubbish!" said the soldier. "Tell me directly what you want with it, or I will draw my sword and cut off your head."

"I won't!" said the witch.

Then the soldier cut off her head; there she lay! But he tied all the money up in her apron, slung it on his back like a pack, put the tinder box in his pocket, and marched off to the town.

It was a beautiful town, and he went straight to the finest hotel, ordered the grandest rooms and all the food he liked best, because he was a rich man now that he had so much money.

Certainly the servant who had to clean his boots thought they were funny old things for such a rich gentleman, but he had not had time yet to buy any new ones; the next day he bought new boots and fine clothes. The soldier now became a fine gentleman, and the people told him all about the grand things in the town, and about their king, and what a lovely princess his daughter was.

"Where is she to be seen?" asked the soldier.

"You can't see her at all!" they all said; "she lives in a great copper castle surrounded with walls and towers. Nobody but the king dare go in and out, for it has been prophesied that she will marry a common soldier, and the king doesn't like that!"

"I should like to see her well enough!" thought the soldier. But there was no way of getting leave for that.

He now led a very merry life; went to theatres, drove about in the King's Park, and gave away a lot of money to poor people, which was very nice of him; for he remembered how disagreeable it used to be not to have a penny in his pocket. Now he was rich, wore fine clothes, and had a great many friends, who all said what a nice fellow he was—a thorough gentleman—and he liked to be told that.

But as he went on spending money every day and his store was never renewed, he at last found himself with only two pence left. Then he was obliged to move out of his fine rooms. He had to take a tiny little attic up under the roof, clean his own boots, and mend them himself with a darning needle. None of his friends went to see him, because there were far too many stairs.

One dark evening when he had not even enough money to buy a candle with, he suddenly remembered that there was a little bit in the old tinder box he had brought out of the hollow tree, when the witch helped him down. He got out the tinder box with the candle end in it and struck fire, but as the sparks flew out from the flint the door burst open and the dog with eyes as big as saucers, which he had seen down under the tree, stood before him and said, "What does my lord command?"

"By heaven!" said the soldier, "this is a nice kind of tinder box, if I can get whatever I want like this! Get me some money," he said to the dog, and away it went.

It was back in a twinkling with a big bag full of pennies in its mouth.

Now the soldier saw what a treasure he had in the tinder box. If he struck once, the dog which sat on the box of copper came; if he struck twice, the dog on the silver box came, and if he struck three times, the one from the box of gold.

He now moved down to the grand rooms and got his fine clothes again, and then all his friends knew him once more and liked him as much as ever.

Then he suddenly began to think: After all, it's a curious thing that no man can get a sight of the princess! Everyone says she is so beautiful! But what is the good of that when she always has to be shut up in that big copper palace with all the towers. Can I not somehow manage to see her? Where is my tinder box? Then he struck the flint, and, whisk, came the dog with eyes as big as saucers.

"It certainly is the middle of the night," said the soldier, "but I am very anxious to see the princess, if only for a single moment."

The dog was out of the door in an instant, and before the soldier had time to think about it, he was back again with the princess. There she was, fast asleep on the dog's back, and she was so lovely that anybody could see that she must be a real princess! The soldier could not help it, but he was obliged to kiss her, for he was a true soldier.

Then the dog ran back again with the princess, but in the morning, when the king and queen were having breakfast, the princess said that she had had such a wonderful dream about a dog and a soldier. She had ridden on the dog's back, and the soldier had kissed her.

"That's a pretty tale," said the queen.

After this an old lady-in-waiting had to sit by her bed at night to see if this was really a dream, or what it could be.

The soldier longed so intensely to see the princess again that at night the dog came to fetch her. He took her up and ran off with her as fast as he could, but the old lady-in-waiting put on her galoshes and ran just as fast behind them; when she saw that they disappeared into a large house, she thought now I know where it is, and made a big cross with chalk on the gate. Then she went home and lay down, and presently the dog came back, too, with the princess. When he saw that there was a cross on the gate, he took a bit of chalk,

too, and made crosses on all the gates in the town; now this was very clever of him, for the lady-in-waiting could not possibly find the gate when there were crosses on all the gates.

Early next morning the king, the queen, the lady-in-waiting, and all the court officials went to see where the princess had been.

"There it is," said the king, when he saw the first door with the cross on it.

"No, my dear husband, it is there," said the queen, who saw another door with a cross on it.

"But there is one, and there is another!" they all cried out.

They soon saw that it was hopeless to try and find it.

Now the queen was a very clever woman; she knew more than how to drive in a chariot. She took her big gold scissors and cut up a large piece of silk into small pieces, and made a pretty little bag, which she filled with fine grains of buckwheat. She then tied it on to the back of the princess, and when that was done she cut a little hole in the bag, so that the grains could drop out all the way wherever the princess went.

At night the dog came again, took the princess on his back, and ran off with her to the soldier, who was so fond of her that he longed to be a prince, so that he might have her for his wife.

The dog never noticed how the grain dropped out all along the road from the palace to the soldier's window, where he ran up the wall with the princess.

In the morning the king and the queen easily saw where their daughter had been, and they seized the soldier and threw him into the dungeons.

There he lay! Oh, how dark and tiresome it was, and then one day they said to him, "Tomorrow you are to be hanged." It was not amusing to be told that, especially as he had left his tinder box behind him at the hotel.

In the morning he could see through the bars in the little window that the people were hurrying out of the town to see him hanged. He heard the drums, and saw the soldiers marching along. All the world was going; among them was a shoemaker's boy in his leather apron and slippers. He was in such a hurry that he lost one of his slippers, and it fell close under the soldier's window where he was peeping out through the bars.

"I say, you boy! Don't be in such a hurry" said the soldier to him. "Nothing will happen till I get there! But if you will run to the house where I used to live, and fetch me my tinder box, you shall have a penny! You must put your best foot foremost!"

The boy was only too glad to have the penny, and tore off to get the tinder box, gave it to the soldier, and—yes now we shall hear.

Outside the town a high scaffold had been raised, and the soldiers were drawn up round about it, as well as crowds of the townspeople. The king and the queen sat upon a beautiful throne exactly opposite the judge and all the councillors.

The soldier mounted the ladder, but when they were about to put the rope round his neck, he said that before undergoing his punishment a criminal was always allowed the gratification of a harmless wish, and he wanted very much to smoke a pipe, as it would be his last pipe in this world.

The king would not deny him this, so the soldier took out his tinder box and struck fire, once, twice, three times, and there were all the dogs. The one with eyes like saucers, the one with eyes like millstones, and the one whose eyes were as big as the Round Tower.

"Help me! Save me from being hanged!" cried the soldier.

And then the dogs rushed at the soldiers and the councillors; they took one by the legs, and another by the nose, and threw them up many fathoms into the air; and when they fell down, they were broken all to pieces.

"I won't!" cried the king, but the biggest dog took both him and the queen and threw them after all the others. Then the soldiers became alarmed, and the people shouted, "Oh! good soldier, you shall be our king, and marry the beautiful princess!"

Then they conducted the soldier to the king's chariot, and all three dogs danced along in front of him and shouted "Hurrah!" The boys all put their fingers in their mouths and whistled, and the soldiers presented arms. The princess came out of the copper palace and became queen, which pleased her very much. The wedding took place in a week, and the dogs all had seats at the table, where they sat staring with all their eyes.

The Travelling Companions

Poor John was very sad, his father was ill and he knew that he could not recover. There was no one else in the little room besides these two; it was quite late at night and the lamp had nearly burnt out.

"You have been a good son, John," said the dying man. "I am sure the Lord will help you on in the world!" and he fixed his mild, gentle eyes upon his son, drew a long breath and passed away so quietly, he only seemed to be asleep. John wept bitterly, for now he had nobody in the world belonging to him, neither father nor mother, sister nor brother. Poor John! he knelt by the bedside and kissed his dead father's hands and shed many tears; but at last his eyes closed, and he fell asleep with his head against the hard bed-post.

He had a wonderful dream; he saw the sun and moon bowing before him, and he saw his father quite well and strong again; he laughed as he always used to laugh when he was very pleased. A lovely girl with a golden crown on her long, beautiful hair, stretched out her hand to John, and his father said, "See what a beautiful bride you have won. She is the loveliest maiden in the world." Then he woke up, and all the beautiful things were gone; his father lay on the bed dead and cold, and there was no one else there, poor John!

The dead man was buried in the following week; John walked close behind the coffin, and he could no longer see his good father who had loved him so much. He heard the earth fall upon the coffin lid, and watched it till only a corner was left, and then the last shovelful fell upon it, and it was entirely hidden. He was so miserable, he felt as if his heart would break.

A beautiful psalm was being sung which brought the tears into his eyes, he wept, and this brought him relief. The sun was shining brightly on the green trees, and seemed to say, "Do not be so sad, John! See how blue the sky is; your good father is up there, and he will pray to God that all may be well with you."

"I will always be good!" said John, "and then I shall go to Heaven some time to my father, and what joy it will be to see each other again. How much I shall have to tell him; and he will have so much to show me, and to teach me about the bliss of Heaven, just as he used to teach me here on earth. Oh, what joy it will be!"

John saw it all so vividly that he smiled at the thought, although the tears still ran down his cheeks. The little birds in the chestnut tree twittered with joy although they had been at the funeral, but they knew that the dead man was in Heaven, and that he now had wings larger and more beautiful than their own. They knew, too, that he was happy, because he had been a good man here on earth, and they were glad of it. John saw them fly away from the trees out into the world, and he felt a strong desire to fly away with them. But first he made a wooden cross to put up on his father's grave; when he brought it along in the evening he found the grave covered with sand and decorated with flowers. This had been done by strangers for love of his father.

Early next morning John packed his little bundle and

stowed away his sole inheritance in his belt; it only consisted of fifty dollars and a few silver coins, and with these he started out into the world. But first he went to the churchyard to his father's grave, where he knelt and said the Lord's prayer, and then added, "Farewell, dear father! I will always be good, and then you won't be afraid to pray to the good God that all may go well with me!"

The fields that John passed through were full of bright flowers nodding their heads in the warm sunshine as much as to say, "Welcome into the fields! Is it not lovely here?" but John turned round once more to look at the old church where he had been baptised, and where he had gone every Sunday and sung the psalms with his good old father. On looking back he saw standing in one of the loop-holes of the tower the little church-Nissé with his pointed red cap, shading his eyes from the sun with his arm. John nodded good-bye to him, and the little Nissé waved his hand and kissed his fingers to him to show that he was sending his good wishes for a pleasant journey.

John now began to think how many beautiful things he would see in the great beautiful world before him, and he went on and on till he found himself much further away than he had ever been before. He did not know the towns through which he passed, or the people he met, he was quite among strangers. The first night he had to sleep under a haystack in a field, for he had no other bed. But he thought it was lovely, no king could have had a better. The field by the river, the haystack, and the deep blue sky above made a charming room. The green grass dotted with red and white flowers was the carpet, the elders and the rose bushes were growing bouquets, and he had the whole river for a bath, with its clear fresh water, and the rushes which nodded their heads bidding him both "Good-night" and "Good-morning." The moon was a great night-light high up under the blue ceiling, one which would never set fire to the curtains. John could sleep quite quietly without fear, and this he also did. He only woke when the sun was high up in the sky and all the little birds were singing, "Good-morning! Good-morning! Are you not up yet?"

The bells were ringing for church; people were on their way to hear the parson pray and preach, and John went with them. He sang a psalm and listened to the word of God, and he felt as if he were in his own old church, where he had been christened, and where he had sung the psalms with his father. There were a great many graves in the churchyard, and some of them were overgrown with long grass. John thought of his father's grave, which some day might look like these when he was no longer there to weed and trim it. So he knelt down, pulled up the long grass, and raised the wooden crosses which had fallen down. He picked up the wreaths which had been blown away and replaced them, thinking that perhaps someone would do the same for his father's grave now he was away.

An old beggar was standing outside the churchyard leaning on a crutch, and John gave him the few silver coins he had left, and then went happily and cheerfully on into the wide world. Towards evening a fearful storm came on and John hurried to get under shelter, but it soon grew dark. At last he reached a little church standing on a solitary hill; the door was ajar, and he slipped in to take shelter till the storm was over.

"I will sit down here in a corner till the storm is over," he said; "I am quite tired and in need of a rest!" so he sat down, folded his hand, and said his evening prayer; and before he was aware he was asleep and dreaming, while it thundered and lightened outside.

When he woke up it was the middle of the night and the storm was over: the moon was shining in upon him through the windows. In the middle of the aisle stood an open coffin with a dead man in it who was not yet buried. John was not at all afraid, for he had a good conscience, and he knew that the dead can do no harm; it is living wicked people who do harm to others. There were two such bad men standing by the coffin. They had come to do harm to this poor dead man; to turn him out of his coffin and throw the body outside the church door.

"Why do you want to do this?" asked John. "It is very wicked and disgraceful; let the man rest for Heaven's sake!"

"Oh nonsense!" replied the wretches; "he cheated us, he owed us money which he could not pay, and now he has gone and died into the bargain, and we shall never see a penny, so we want to revenge ourselves. He shall lie like a dog outside the church doors!"

"I have not got more than fifty dollars," said John: "it is my whole inheritance, but I will gladly give it to you if you will honestly promise me to leave the poor dead man in peace. I shall manage very well without the money, I have good strong limbs, and the Lord will always help me."

"Well," said the bad men, "if you are ready to pay his debt like that, we won't do him any harm, we can assure you!"

And they took the money John gave them, laughing at him for being such a simpleton, and then they went away. John put the body straight again, folded the hands, said good-bye, and went away through the woods in a state of great satisfaction. Around him, where the moon pierced through the trees, he saw numbers of little elves playing about merrily. They did not disturb themselves on his account, they knew very well that he was a good innocent person, and it is only bad people who never see the fairies. Some of them were no bigger than one's finger, and they had long yellow hair fastened up with golden combs. They swung hand in hand upon the big dewdrops which covered the leaves and the long grass. Sometimes the dewdrops rolled down, and then they fell with it down among the grass, and this caused great noise and laughter among the little folks. It was very amusing. They sang all the pretty little songs John used to know when he was a little boy. Great spiders with silver crowns upon their heads spun their webs from branch to branch like bridges connecting palaces. They glittered in the moonlight like glass where the dew had fallen on them. They went on with their sports till the sun rose, and the little creatures crept away into the flower buds, and the wind caught the bridges and palaces and swept them away into the air like cobwebs.

John had just got through the wood, when a strong man's voice called out behind him, "Hallo, comrade! whither away?"

"Out into the wide world," said John. "I have neither father nor mother, I am only a poor lad, but the Lord will protect me."

"I am going out into the wide world too!" said the stranger; "shall we go together?"

"By all means," said John, and so they walked on together.

They soon grew much attached to each other, for they were both good men, but John soon saw that the stranger was

much wiser than himself, he had been round the greater part
of the world, and he was well able to describe all he had seen.

The sun was already high when they sat down under a big
tree to eat their breakfast, and just then an old woman came
up. She was very old and bent, and walked with a crutch; she
had a bundle of sticks she had picked up in the wood on her
back, and her apron was fastened up, and John could see in
it three bundles or faggots of dried fern and some willow
twigs. When she got near them, her foot slipped and she fell
with a loud shriek; the poor old woman had broken her leg.

John wanted to carry her home, but the stranger opened his
knapsack, and took out a little pot of salve, which he said
would make her leg well directly, and she would be able to
walk home as well as if she had never broken it. But in payment for it he wanted the three bundles of fern she had in her
apron.

"That is very good payment," said the old woman, nodding
her head rather oddly; she did not want to part with her
three bundles of fern, but it was not so pleasant to lie there
with a broken leg, so she gave him the faggots. As soon as he
had rubbed on the salve, the old woman got up and walked
away faster than she had been able to do before. This was
all the effect of the salve; but no such ointment as this was to
be had at any chemist's.

"Whatever do you want with those bundles of fern?" said
John to his companion.

"They make very good birch rods, and they are just what I
like. I am a very queer fellow, you know!"

Then they walked on for a good bit.

"What a storm is drawing up there!" said John, pointing
before him; "those are terribly black clouds."

"No," said his fellow-traveller, "those are not clouds, they are mountains, beautiful high mountains, where you can get right above the clouds into the fresh air. It is splendid up there! Tomorrow we shall just reach them."

They were not so near, however, as they seemed to be; it took them a whole day to reach the mountains, where the dark forests grew right up towards the sky, and where there were great boulders as big as houses, or even towns. It would be a heavy task to climb over all these, and so John and his fellow traveller went into an inn to rest and refresh themselves before they made the ascent next day. There were a number of people in the parlour at the inn, for there was a man showing off some marionettes. He had just put up his little theatre, and the people were sitting round waiting for the play to begin. A fat old butcher had taken up his place in the middle of the front row, and he had a ferocious looking bulldog by his side, and it sat staring just as hard as anybody else.

Then the comedy began, and it was a very pretty play, with a King and a Queen in it. They sat on a velvet throne with golden crowns on their heads, and trains, for they could well afford it. The prettiest little wooden dolls stood by all the doors, they had bright glass eyes and big whiskers, and they were employed in opening and shutting the doors to let in the fresh air. It was a capital play, and not at all a tragic one, but just as the Queen got up to walk across the floor—Heaven knows what idea entered the bulldog's head, but finding that the butcher was not holding him, he made a great leap forward right into the middle of the theatre and seized the Queen by the slender waist, and crunched her head up. It was a terrible disaster!

The poor showman was quite frightened and also very sad

about his Queen, for she was his prettiest doll, and the horrid bulldog had entirely ruined her. But when all the people had gone away John's fellow-traveller said he could make her all right again, and he took out his little pot and rubbed some of the same ointment on to the doll which had cured the poor old woman who had broken her leg. As soon as ever the doll had been rubbed over with the ointment she became whole again, nay, she could even move all her limbs herself; it was no longer necessary to pull the wires. The doll was exactly like a living being, except that she could not speak. The showman was delighted, because now he did not have to hold the wires at all for this doll, as she could dance quite well by herself, and none of the others could do that.

At night, when everybody had gone to bed, someone was heard sighing most dolefully, and it went on so long that everybody got up to see who it could be. The showman went along to his theatre, because that was where the sighs seemed to come from. All the wooden dolls were lying in a heap; it was the King and his guards who were sighing so dismally and staring with their glass eyes. They all wanted to be rubbed with some of the same ointment as the Queen, so that they might be able to move their limbs as well as she did. She threw herself down on her knees and stretched out her hands with her golden crown, saying, "Pray, take this, but do, please, rub some of the ointment on to my consort and the courtiers!" The poor man who owned the theatre and the marionettes could not help crying, he was so sorry for them. He immediately promised the travelling-companion that he would give him all the money he possessed if he would only anoint five or six of the prettiest dolls. But the travelling-companion said that he did not want anything except the big

sword that the showman wore at his side, and as soon as it
was given him he anointed six dolls. They began to dance
about at once so prettily that all the real, living girls who
saw them began to dance too. The coachman and the cook,
the waiter and the chambermaid, and all the strangers joined
in, as well as the shovel and the tongs: but those two fell on
the top of each other just as they were making their first
bound. It was indeed a lively night!

Next morning John and his travelling-companion went away
from them all, up the high mountains and through the great
pine forests. They got so high that at last the church towers
far below looked like little red berries among all the green;
and they could see far away for many, many miles, to places
where they had never been! John had never seen so many of
the beauties of this beautiful world all together before. The
warm sun shone brightly in the clear blue sky, and the hunts-
man was heard winding his horn among the mountains; it was
all so peaceful and sweet that it brought tears to his eyes, and
he could not help exclaiming, "Great God, I could fall down
and kiss the hem of Thy garment out of gratitude for all Thy
good gifts to us!"

His travelling-companion also stood with folded hands looking at the woods and the villages basking in the warm sunshine. They heard a wonderful and beautiful sound above
their heads, and looked up; a great white swan was hovering
in the air above them. It sang as they had never heard any
bird sing before; but the song became fainter and fainter,
and the swan gradually sank down before their feet, where it
lay dead—the beautiful bird.

"Two such beautiful wings," said the travelling-companion.
"Such big white ones are worth a lot of money; I will take

them with me. Now, you see what a good thing it was that I got this sword!" and with one blow he struck off both the wings of the dead swan, for he meant to keep them.

They travelled many, many miles over the mountains, till at last they saw before them a great town with over a hundred towers, which glittered like silver in the sunshine. In the middle of the town was a splendid marble palace, thatched with red gold, in which the King lived.

John and his travelling-companion did not want to go into the town at once; they stopped at an inn outside to change their clothes, as they wished to look their best when they walked through the streets. The host told them that the King was such a good old man, he never did any harm to anyone; but his daughter—Heaven preserve us! she was a wicked Princess.

Beauty she had more than enough of; nobody could be so beautiful and fascinating as she was, but what was the good of it when she was such a bad, wicked witch, who was the cause of so many handsome Princes having lost their lives. She had given permission to anybody to court her. Anyone who would might come, were he Prince or beggar—it was all the same to her; he only had to guess three riddles she asked him. If he could answer them, she would marry him, and he would be king over all the land when her father died; but if he failed to answer them, he either had to be hanged or to have his head cut off. So bad and so wicked was this beautiful Princess. Her father, the old King, was much grieved by it, but he could not prevent her from being so wicked, for he had once said that he would never have anything to do with her lovers; she must deal with them herself as she liked. Every Prince who had yet come to guess the riddles so as to gain the Princess had failed, and so he had either been hanged or had his head cut off. Each one had been warned, and he need not have paid his addresses unless he had liked. The old King was so grieved by all this trouble and misery that he and his soldiers spent a whole day every year on their knees praying that the Princess might become good. But she had no intention of so doing. The old women who drank brandy dyed it black before they drank it; that was their way of mourning, and what more could they do!

"That vile Princess!" said John, "she ought to be well birched, that would be the best thing for her. If I were the King I would make the blood run!" Just then they heard all the people in the streets shouting "Hurrah!" The Princess was passing, and she was really so beautiful that when they saw her everybody forgot how wicked she was, and so they all shouted "Hurrah." Twelve beautiful maidens clothed in white silk, with golden tulips in their hands, rode twelve coal-black horses by her side. The Princess herself was on a snow-white horse, adorned with diamonds and rubies; her riding dress was of pure gold, and the whip in her hand looked like a sunbeam. The golden crown on her head seemed to be made of little twinkling stars from the sky; and her cloak was sewn all over with thousands of beautiful butterflies' wings. But she was far, far more beautiful than all her clothes.

When John saw her his face became as red as blood, and he could hardly say a single word; the Princess was the image of the beautiful girl with the golden crown whom he had seen in his dream the night his father died. He thought her so beautiful that he at once fell in love with her. It certainly could not be true, he thought, that she could be a wicked witch who allowed people to be hanged or executed if they could not guess her riddles. "Anyone may pay his addresses to her, even the poorest peasant: I will go to the Palace myself! I can't help going!"

They all said that he ought not to go as he would only meet the same fate as the others. His travelling-companion also advised him against going, but John thought he would be sure to get on all right; so he brushed his coat and his shoes, washed his hands and face, and combed his yellow hair, and then went quite alone to the town and straight up to the Palace.

"Come in," said the old King when John knocked at the door. He opened it, and the old King in his dressing-gown and slippers came towards him. He had his gold crown on his head, the sceptre in one hand, and the golden ball in the other. "Wait a moment," said he, tucking the ball under his arm so as to be able to shake hands with John. But as soon as he heard that John was a suitor he began to cry so much that both the ball and the sceptre rolled on to the floor, and he had to wipe his eyes with his dressing-gown. The poor old King!

"Leave it alone!" said he; "you are sure to fail just like the others, I am convinced of it!" Then he led John into the Princess' pleasure garden, which was a ghastly sight. From every tree hung three or four King's sons who had come to court the Princess, but who had all been unable to guess her riddles. With every gust of wind the bones rattled so that all the little birds were frightened away and they never dared come into the garden; all the flowers were tied up to human bones in the place of stakes, and human skulls grinned out of every flower pot. It was indeed a nice garden for a Princess.

"Here you see," said the old King, "your fate will be just

the same as all these. Do give it up. It makes me most unhappy, I take it so much to heart." John kissed the old King's
hand and said he thought it would be all right for he was so
fond of the beautiful Princess.

Just then the Princess came herself with all her ladies driving into the Palace gardens, so they went up to her and said
"Good-morning." She was certainly very beautiful as she
shook hands with John, and he was more in love with her
than ever; it was impossible that she could be the wicked
witch people said she was. They all went up into the hall and
the little pages brought jam and gingerbread nuts to them;
but the old King was so sad that he could eat nothing, besides the ginger nuts were too hard for him.

It was now decided that John was to come up to the Palace
the next morning, when the judges and all the council would
be assembled to hear if he could guess the first riddle. If he
succeeded the first time, he would have to come twice more,
but nobody yet had ever guessed the first riddle—he had lost
his life at once.

John was not a bit alarmed about himself; he was delighted,
and only thought of the lovely Princess. He felt quite certain
that the good God would help him, but in what manner it
would be he had not the slightest idea, nor did he trouble his
head about it. He danced along the highway, when he went
back to the inn where his travelling-companion was waiting
for him. John was never tired of telling him how charming the
Princess had been towards him, and how lovely she was. He
was longing for the next day to come, when he was to go to
the Palace to try his luck with the riddles. But his travelling-
companion shook his head and was quite sad.

"I am so fond of you," he said; "we might have been com-

panions for a long time yet, and now I shall lose you directly!
My poor dear John, I could weep over you, but I will not
spoil your pleasure on the last evening we perhaps may spend
together. We will be merry, as merry as possible; tomorrow
when you are gone I can be sad!"

Everybody in the town had heard directly that a new suitor
had come for the Princess, and there was general mourning.
The theatre was closed, and all the cakewomen tied black
crape round the sugar pigs. The King and the priests were
praying on their knees in the churches, and there was universal grief, for they all knew that there could be no better fate
in store for John than for the other suitors.

Late in the evening the travelling-companion made a great
bowl of punch, and said to John that they must be merry now
and drink the Princess' health. But when John had drunk two
glasses he became so sleepy that he could not hold up his
head, and he fell fast asleep. His travelling-companion lifted
him quietly up from his chair, and laid him on his bed. As
soon as it was dark he took the two big wings which he had
cut off the swan, and tied them on to his own shoulders; then
he put the biggest bunch of twigs he had got from the old
woman who had broken her leg into his pocket, opened the
window, and flew over the roofs of the houses right up to the
Palace, where he sat down in a corner under the window of the
Princess' bedroom.

The whole town was quiet. As the clock struck the quarter
before twelve the window was opened, and the Princess flew
out in a great white cloak and long black wings. She flew over
the town to a great mountain, but the travelling-companion
made himself invisible and flew behind her, raining blows on
her back with his birch rod, till the blood flowed. Oh, what a

flight that was through the air; the wind caught her cloak, which spread out on every side like the sail of a ship, and the moon shone through it.

"How it hails, how it hails!" said the Princess at every blow, but she richly deserved it.

At last they reached the mountain and knocked; there was a rumble as of thunder, the side of the mountain opened, and the Princess went in, closely followed by the travelling-companion. No one saw him, as he was quite invisible. They went through a long passage which glittered curiously, owing to thousands of shining spiders which swarmed over the walls, shedding a fiery light. They next reached a great hall built of gold and silver, with red and blue flowers as big as sunflowers all over the walls. No one could pick these flowers, for the stems were poisonous snakes, and the flowers were flames coming out of their mouths. The ceiling was covered with shining glow-worms and pale blue bats which flapped their transparent wings. This had an extraordinary effect. In the middle of the floor was a throne supported on four horses' legs with harness of the red fiery spiders. The throne itself was of milky glass, and the cushions were made of little black mice holding on to each other by the tails. There was a canopy above it of rose-coloured spider's web, dotted with the most exquisite little green flies which glittered like diamonds.

A hideous old ogre sat in the middle of the throne with a crown on his ugly head and a sceptre in his hand. He kissed the Princess on her forehead, and made her sit down by him on the costly throne, then the music began! Great black grasshoppers played upon Jews' harps, and the owl beat upon his own stomach in place of a drum. It was a most absurd concert. Numbers of tiny little elves, each with a firefly on their little caps, danced round the hall. No one could see the travelling-companion, but he could see and hear everything from behind the throne, where he had placed himself. The courtiers who now made their appearance looked most grand and proper, but anyone who could really see perceived at once what they were. They were merely broomsticks with cabbages for heads, into which the ogre had put life by his magic powers and dressed them up in embroidered clothes. But this did not matter a bit, for they were only used on grand occasions.

After the dancing had gone on for a time, the Princess told the ogre that she had another suitor, and asked him what she had better think of to put as a riddle the next day.

"Listen!" said the ogre; "I will tell you what, you must think of something very simple, and then he will never think of it. Let us say one of your own shoes; he will never guess that. Then have his head chopped off, but don't forget when you come here to-morrow night to bring me his eyes. I want to eat them."

The Princess curtsied low, and said that she would not forget the eyes. The ogre opened the mountain, and she flew home again; and, as before, the travelling-companion followed her closely and beat her so hard with the birch rod that she groaned at the terrible hailstorm and hurried back as fast as she could to her bedroom window. The travelling-companion flew back to the inn, where he found John still fast asleep. He took off his own clothes and went to bed too, for he had good right to be tired.

John woke up early in the morning, and the travelling-companion got up at the same time, and told him that he had had a wonderful dream about the Princess and her shoe; and he begged John to ask the Princess if she had not thought of her shoe. This was of course what he had heard the ogre say in the mountain, but he did not want to tell John anything about that, and so he merely told him it was a dream.

"I may just as well ask that as anything else!" said John, "perhaps your dream will come true, for I always think God will help me! All the same I will say good-bye, for if I guess wrong you will never see me again."

So they kissed each other, and John went to the town and up to the Palace. The hall was full of people; the judges were seated in their arm-chairs, and they had down pillows under their heads for they had so much to think about. The old King stood near wiping his eyes with a white pocket handkerchief. Then the Princess came in, greeting everyone very pleasantly, and she was even lovelier than yesterday. She shook hands with John and said, "Good-morning to you." Now John had to guess what she had thought of. She looked at him most sweetly, but as soon as she heard him say the word shoe, she turned as white as a sheet and trembled all over; but that was no good, for he had guessed aright.

Preserve us! how pleased the old King was, he turned head over hells without stopping, and everybody clapped their hands both on his account and on John's, whose first guess had been right.

The travelling-companion beamed with delight when he heard how successful John had been. Bu John folded his hands and thanked God, who no doubt would also help him on the two following occasions. The next day was fixed for the second riddle.

The evening passed just as the previous one had done. When John had gone to sleep the travelling-companion flew behind the Princess to the mountain, and he beat her harder than ever, for this time he had taken two birch rods with him. Nobody could see him, and he heard everything as before. The Princess was to think of her glove, and this he told John just as if it had been a dream. John of course could easily guess aright, and again there was great delight at the Palace. The whole court turned somersaults, as they had seen the King do the first time; but the Princess lay on the sofa and would not say a single word. Now all turned upon whether John guessed the third riddle or not. If he did, he would win the Princess and inherit the whole kingdom when the old King died; but if he was wrong, he would lose his life, and the ogre would eat his beautiful blue eyes.

The evening before, John went early to bed, said his prayers, and slept as peacefully as possible; but the travelling companion tied the wings on to his back, and bound the sword round his waist, took all the birch rods, and flew off to the Palace.

It was a pitch dark night. There was such a gale that the tiles flew off the roofs, and the trees in the garden of bones bent like reeds before the wind. The lightning flashed every moment, and the thunder rolled continuously the whole night long. The window burst open and the Princess flew out; she was as pale as death, but she laughed at the storm as if it were not bad enough; her white mantle swirled about in the wind like the sails of a ship. The travelling-companion beat her with his three birches till the blood dripped on to the ground. She could hardly fly any further. At last they reached the mountain.

"What a hailstorm there is!" she said as she entered. "I have never been out in such a bad one!"

"One may have too much of a good thing!" said the ogre.

Then she told him that John's second guess had been right, and if he was successful again in the morning she would never be able to come and see him again in the mountain. Nor would she ever be able to do any more of the sorcerer's tricks as before, and she was very sad about it.

"He shall never guess it," said the ogre.

"I shall think of something that will never enter his head. But we will have some fun first!" And he took the Princess by both hands and they danced round the room with all the little elves and the fireflies. The red spiders ran merrily up and down the walls, and the fire flowers seemed to give out sparks. The owls played their drums, the crickets chirped, and the grasshoppers played their harps. It was a very gay ball.

After they had danced some time the Princess was obliged to go home or she would be missed, and the ogre said he would go with her so as to have more of her company.

So away they flew through the storm, and the travelling-companion wore out his birch rods on their backs; never had the ogre been out in such a hailstorm. He said good-bye to the Princess outside the Palace, and whispered to her, "Think of my head," but the travelling-companion heard what he said, and at the very moment when the Princess slipped in at her window, and the ogre was turning away to go back, he seized him by his long black beard, and before he had time to look round, cut off his head close to the shoulders with his big sword. He threw the body into the sea to be food for fishes, but he only dipped the head into the water, and tied it up in his silk handkerchief and took it back to the inn, and he then went to bed.

Next morning he gave John the handkerchief, but said he

must not open it before the Princess asked him what she had thought about.

There were so many people in the hall that they were packed as close together as a bundle of radishes. The judges were sitting in their arm-chairs with the soft down cushions; and the old King had his new clothes on, and his crown and sceptre had been polished up and looked quite festive. But the Princess was very, very pale, and she was dressed in black, as if for a funeral.

"What have I thought of?" she asked John; and he immediately untied the handkerchief, and was very much frightened himself when he saw the hideous ogre's head. A shudder ran through the whole assemblage, but the Princess seemed turned to stone, and could not say a single word. At last she got up and gave her hand to John, for he had guessed all the riddles; she looked neither to the right nor to the left, but sighed deeply, and said, "You are my master now; our wedding shall take place to-night." "I like that," said the old King; "that is just as it should be." All the people shouted hurrah, the guard's band played in the streets, the bells rang, and the cakewomen took the crape off the sugar pigs, because all was now rejoicing. Three oxen stuffed with chickens and ducks were roasted whole in the market-place, and everyone could cut off a portion for themselves. The fountains played wine instead of water, and anyone who bought a penny roll had six large buns full of plums given him.

In the evening the whole town was illuminated. The soldiers fired salutes, and the boys let off squibs and crackers. At the Palace all was eating and drinking, toasting and dancing. The grand gentlemen danced with the pretty ladies, and the singing could be heard far and wide.

But the Princess was still bewitched, and she did not care a bit about John; the travelling-companion knew this, and gave him three feathers out of the swan's wings and a little bottle with a few drops of liquid in it. He told John to have a large bath full of water placed by the side of the bed and when the Princess was going to get into bed he must give her a little push so that she fell into the water, where he was to dip her three times, first having thrown the three feathers and the drops of liquid into it. She would then be released from the spell and would grow very fond of him.

John did everything as he was told. The Princess shrieked when he dipped her into the water, and struggled in his hands in the form of a black swan with glittering eyes. The second time she came up as a white swan, except for a black ring round the neck. John prayed humbly to God, and the third time she came up as a lovely Princess. She was more lovely than she had been before, and thanked him, with tears in her eyes, for having released her from the spell.

Next morning the old King came with all his courtiers to offer their congratulations, and this went on all day. Last of all came the travelling-companion; he had his stick in his hand and his knapsack on his back. John kissed him over and over, and said that he must not go away, he must stay with them, as he was the cause of all their happiness. But the travelling-companion shook his head and said gently and tenderly, "No; my time is up. I have only paid my debt. Do you remember the dead man whom you prevented the wicked men from disturbing. You gave all that you possessed so that he might have rest in his grave. I am the dead man!" And then he immediately vanished.

The wedding festivities lasted a whole month. John and

the Princess were devoted to each other, and the old King had many happy days in which to let their little children play "ride a cock-horse" on his knee and to play with his sceptre. But John was King over the whole country.

The Ugly Duckling

The country was lovely just then; it was summer. The wheat was golden and the oats still green; the hay was stacked in the rich low-lying meadows, where the stork was marching about on his long red legs, chattering Egyptian, the language his mother had taught him.

Round about field and meadow lay great woods, in the midst of which were deep lakes. Yes, the country certainly was delicious. In the sunniest spot stood an old mansion surrounded by a deep moat, and great dock leaves grew from the walls of the house right down to the water's edge; some of them were so tall that a small child could stand upright under them. In amongst the leaves it was as secluded as in the depths of a forest; and there a duck was sitting on her nest. Her little ducklings were just about to be hatched, but she was nearly tired of sitting, for it had lasted such a long time. Moreover, she had very few visitors, as the other ducks liked swimming about in the moat better than waddling up to sit under the dock leaves and gossip with her.

At last one egg after another began to crack. "Cheep, cheep!" they said. All the chicks had come to life, and were poking their heads out.

"Quack! quack!" said the duck; and then they all quacked their hardest, and looked about them on all sides among the green leaves; their mother allowed them to look as much as they liked, for green is good for the eyes.

"How big the world is, to be sure!" said all the young ones; for they certainly had ever so much more room to move about than when they were inside in the egg shell.

"Do you imagine this is the whole world?" said the mother. "It stretches a long way on the other side of the garden, right into the parson's field; but I have never been as far as that! I suppose you are all here now?" and she got up. "No! I declare I have not got you all yet! The biggest egg is still there; how long is it going to last?" and then she settled herself on the nest again.

"Well, how are you getting on?" said an old duck who had come to pay her a visit.

"This one egg is taking such a long time," answered the sitting duck, "the shell will not crack; but now you must look at the others; they are the finest ducklings I have ever seen! they are all exactly like their father, the rascal! he never comes to see me."

"Let me look at the egg which won't crack," said the old duck. "You may be sure that it is a turkey's egg! I have been cheated like that once, and I had no end of trouble and worry with the creatures, for I may tell you that they are afraid of the water. I could not get them into it, I quacked and snapped at them, but it was no good. Let me see the egg! Yes, it is a turkey's egg! You just leave it alone and teach the other children to swim."

"I will sit on it a little longer, I have sat so long already, that I may as well go on till the Midsummer Fair comes round."

"Please yourself," said the old duck, and she went away.

At last the big egg cracked. "Cheep, cheep!" said the young one and tumbled out; how big and ugly he was!

The duck looked at him. "That is a monstrous big duckling," she said; "none of the others looked like that; can he be a turkey chick? well we shall soon find that out; into the water he shall go, if I have to kick him in myself."

Next day was gloriously fine, and the sun shone on all the green dock leaves. The mother duck with her whole family went down to the moat.

Splash, into the water she sprang. "Quack, quack!" she said, and one duckling plumped in after the other. The water dashed over their heads, but they came up again and floated beautifully; their legs went of themselves, and they were all there, even the big ugly grey one swam about with them.

"No, that is no turkey," she said; "she how beautifully he uses his legs and how erect he holds himself: he is my own chick! after all, he is not so bad when you come to look at him properly. Quack, quack! Now come with me and I will take you into the world, and introduce you to the duckyard; but keep close to me all the time, so that no one may tread upon you, and beware of the cat!"

Then they went into the duckyard. There was a fearful uproar going on, for two broods were fighting for the head of an eel, and in the end the cat captured it.

"That's how things go in this world," said the mother duck, and she licked her bill, for she wanted the eel's head herself.

"Use your legs," said she; "mind you quack properly, and bend your necks to the old duck over there! She is the grandest of them all; she has Spanish blood in her veins and that accounts for her size, and, do you see? she has a red rag round her leg; that is a wonderfully fine thing, and the most extraordinary mark of distinction any duck can have. It shows clearly that she is not to be parted with, and that she is worthy of recognition both by beasts and men! Quack now! don't turn your toes in, a well brought up duckling keeps his legs wide apart just like father and mother; that's it, now bend your necks, and say quack!"

They did as they were bid, but the other ducks round about looked at them and said, quite loud; "Just look there! now we are to have that tribe! just as if there were not enough of us already, and, oh dear! how ugly that duckling is, we won't stand him!" and a duck flew at him at once and bit him in the neck.

"Let him be," said the mother; "he is doing no harm."

"Very likely not, but he is so ungainly and queer," said the biter; "he must be whacked."

"They are handsome children mother has," said the old duck with the rag round her leg; "all good looking except this one, and he is not a good specimen; it's a pity you can't make him over again."

"That can't be done, your grace," said the mother duck: "he is not handsome, but he is a thorough good creature, and he swims as beautifully as any of the others; nay, I think I might venture even to add that I think he will improve as he goes on, or perhaps in time he may grow smaller! He was too long in the egg, and so he has not come out with a very good figure." And then she patted his neck and stroked him down. "Besides he is a drake," said she; "so it does not matter so much. I believe he will be very strong, and I don't doubt but he will make his way in the world."

"The other ducklings are very pretty," said the old duck. "Now make yourselves quite at home, and if you find the head of an eel you may bring it to me!"

After that they felt quite at home. But the poor duckling which had been the last to come out of the shell, and who was so ugly, was bitten, pushed about, and made fun of both by the ducks and the hens. "He is too big," they all said; and the turkey-cock, who was born with his spurs on, and therefore thought himself quite an emperor, puffed himself up like a vessel in full sail, made for him, and gobbled and gobbled till he became quite red in the face. The poor duckling was at his wit's end, and did not know which way to turn; he was in despair because he was so ugly, and the butt of the whole duckyard.

So the first day passed, and afterwards matters grew worse and worse. The poor duckling was chased and hustled by all of them, even his brothers and sisters ill-used him; and they were always saying, "If only the cat would get hold of you, you hideous object!" Even his mother said, "I wish to goodness you were miles away." The ducks bit him, the hens pecked him, and the girl who fed them kicked him aside.

Then he ran off and flew right over the hedge, where the little birds flew up into the air in a fright.

"That is because I am so ugly," thought the poor duckling, shutting his eyes, but he ran on all the same. Then he came to a great marsh where the wild ducks lived; he was so tired and miserable that he stayed there the whole night.

In the morning the wild ducks flew up to inspect their new comrade.

"What sort of a creature are you?" they inquired, as the duckling turned from side to side and greeted them as well as he could. "You are frightfully ugly," said the wild ducks, "but that does not matter to us, so long as you do not marry into our family!" Poor fellow! he had no thought of marriage, all he wanted was permission to lie among the rushes, and to drink a little of the marsh water.

He stayed there two whole days, then two wild geese came, or rather two wild ganders, they were not long out of the shell, and therefore rather pert.

"I say, comrade," they said, "you are so ugly that we have taken quite a fancy to you; will you join us and be a bird of passage? There is another marsh close by, and there are some charming wild geese there; all sweet young ladies, who can say quack! You are ugly enough to make your fortune among them." Just at that moment, bang! bang! was heard up above, and both the wild geese fell dead among the reeds, and the water turned blood red. Bang! bang! went the guns, and whole flocks of wild geese flew up from the rushes and the shot peppered among them again.

There was a grand shooting party, and the sportsmen lay hidden round the marsh, some even sat on the branches of the trees which overhung the water; the blue smoke rose like clouds among the dark trees and swept over the pool.

The water-dogs wandered about in the swamp, splash! splash! The rushes and reeds bent beneath their tread on all sides. It was terribly alarming to the poor duckling. He twisted his head round to get it under his wing, and just at that moment a frightful, big dog appeared close beside him; his tongue hung right out of his mouth and his eyes glared wickedly. He opened his great chasm of a mouth close to the duckling, showed his sharp teeth—and—splash—went on without touching him.

"Oh, thank Heaven!" sighed the duckling, "I am so ugly that even the dog won't bite me!"

Then he lay quite still while the shot whistled among the bushes, and bang after bang rent the air. It only became quiet late in the day, but even then the poor duckling did not dare to get up; he waited several hours more before he looked about, and then he hurried away from the marsh as fast as he could. He ran across fields and meadows, and there was such a wind that he had hard work to make his way.

Towards night he reached a poor little cottage; it was such a miserable hovel that it could not make up its mind which way to fall even, and so it remained standing. The wind whistled so fiercely round the duckling that he had to sit on his tail to resist it, and it blew harder and harder; then he saw that the door had fallen off one hinge and hung so crookedly that he could creep into the house through the crack, and by this means he made his way into the room. An old woman lived there with her cat and her hen. The cat, which she called "Sonnie," could arch his back, purr, and give off electric sparks, that is to say if you stroked his fur the wrong way. The hen had quite tiny short legs, and so she was called "Chuckie-low-legs." She laid good eggs, and the old woman was as fond of her as if she had been her own child.

In the morning the strange duckling was discovered immediately, and the cat began to purr, and the hen to cluck.

"What on earth is that!" said the old woman looking round, but her sight was not good, and she thought the duckling was a fat duck which had escaped. "This is a capital find," said she; "now I shall have duck's eggs if only it is not a drake! we must find out about that!"

So she took the duckling on trial for three weeks, but no eggs made their appearance. The cat was the master of the house and the hen the mistress, and they always spoke of "we and the world," for they thought that they represented the half of the world, and that quite the better half.

The duckling thought there might be two opinions on the subject, but the cat would not hear of it.

"Can you lay eggs?" she asked.

"No!"

"Will you have the goodness to hold your tongue then!"

And the cat said, "Can you arch your back, purr, or give off sparks?"

"No."

"Then you had better keep your opinions to yourself when people of sense are speaking!"

The duckling sat in the corner nursing his ill-humour; then he began to think of the fresh air and the sunshine, an uncontrollable longing seized him to float on the water, and at last he could not help telling then hen about it.

"What on earth possesses you?" she asked; "you have nothing to do, that is why you get these freaks into your head. Lay some eggs or take to purring, and you will get over it."

"But it is so delicious to float on the water," said the duckling; "so delicious to feel it rushing over your head when you dive to the bottom."

"That would be a fine amusement," said the hen. "I think you have gone mad. Ask the cat about it, he is the wisest creature I know; ask him if he is fond of floating on the water or diving under it. I say nothing about myself. Ask our mistress yourself, the old woman, there is no one in the world cleverer than she is. Do you suppose she has any desire to float on the water, or to duck underneath it?"

"You do not understand me," said the duckling.

"Well, if we don't understand you, who should? I suppose you don't consider yourself cleverer than the cat or the old woman, not to mention me. Don't make a fool of yourself, child, and thank your stars for all the good we have done you! Have you not lived in this warm room, and in such society that you might have learnt something? But you are an idiot, and there is no pleasure in associating with you. You may believe me I mean you well, I tell you home truths, and there is no surer way than that of knowing who are one's friends. You just see about laying some eggs, or learn to purr, or to emit sparks."

"I think I will go out into the wide world," said the duckling.

"Oh, do so by all means," said the hen.

So away went the duckling, he floated on the water and ducked underneath it, but he was looked askance at by every living creature for his ugliness. Now the autumn came on, the leaves in the woods turned yellow and brown; the wind took hold of them, and they danced about. The sky looked very cold, and the clouds hung heavy with snow and hail. A raven stood on the fence and croaked Caw! caw! from sheer cold; it made one shiver only to think of it, the poor duckling certainly was in a bad case.

One evening, the sun was just setting in wintry splendour, when a flock of beautiful large birds appeared out of the bushes; the duckling had never seen anything so beautiful. They were dazzlingly white with long waving necks; they were swans, and uttering a peculiar cry they spread out their magnificent broad wings and flew away from the cold regions to warmer lands and open seas. They mounted so high, so very high, and the ugly little duckling became strangely uneasy, he circled round and round in the water like a wheel, craning his neck up into the air after them. Then he uttered a shriek so piercing and so strange, that he was quite frightened by it himself. Oh, he could not forget those beautiful birds, those happy birds, and as soon as they were out of sight he ducked right down to the bottom, and when he came up again he was quite beside himself. He did not know what the birds were, or whither they flew, but all the same he was more drawn towards them than he had ever been by any creatures before. He did not envy them in the least, how could it occur to him even to wish to be such a marvel of beauty; he would have been thankful if only the ducks would have tolerated him among them—the poor ugly creature!

The winter was so bitterly cold that the duckling was obliged to swim about in the water to keep it from freezing, but every night the hole in which he swam got smaller and smaller. Then it froze so hard that the surface ice cracked, and the duckling had to use his legs all the time, so that the ice should not close in round him; at last he was so weary that he could move no more, and he was frozen fast into the ice.

Early in the morning a peasant came along and saw him; he went out on to the ice and hammered a hole in it with his heavy wooden shoe, and carried the duckling home to his wife. There it soon revived. The children wanted to play with it, but the duckling thought they were going to ill-use him, and rushed in his fright into the milk pan, and the milk spurted out all over the room. The woman shrieked and threw up her hands, then it flew into the butter cask, and down into the meal tub and out again. Just imagine what it looked like by this time! The woman screamed and tried to hit it with the tongs, and the children tumbled over one another in trying to catch it, and they screamed with laughter—by good luck the door stood open, and the duckling flew out among the bushes and the new fallen snow—and it lay there thoroughly exhausted.

But it would be too sad to mention all the privation and misery it had to go through during that hard winter. When the sun began to shine warmly again, the duckling was in the marsh, lying among the rushes; the larks were singing and the beautiful spring had come.

Then all at once it raised its wings and they flapped with much greater strength than before, and bore him off vigorously. Before he knew where he was, he found himself in a large garden where the apple trees were in full blossom, and the air was scented with lilacs, the long branches of which overhung the indented shores of the lake! Oh! the spring freshness was so delicious!

Just in front of him he saw three beautiful white swans advancing towards him from a thicket; with rustling feathers they swam lightly over the water. The duckling recognised the majestic birds, and he was overcome by a strange melancholy.

"I will fly to them, the royal birds, and they will hack me to pieces, because I, who am so ugly, venture to approach them! But it won't matter; better be killed by them than be snapped at by the ducks, pecked by the hens, or spurned by the henwife, or suffer so much misery in the winter."

So he flew into the water and swam towards the stately swans; they saw him and darted towards him with ruffled feathers.

"Kill me, oh, kill me!" said the poor creature, and bowing his head towards the water he awaited his death. But what did he see reflected in the transparent water?

He saw below him his own image, but he was no longer a clumsy dark grey bird, ugly and ungainly, he was himself a swan! It does not matter in the least having been born in a duckyard, if only you come out of a swan's egg!

He felt quite glad of all the misery and tribulation he had gone through; he was the better able to appreciate his good fortune now, and all the beauty which greeted him. The big swans swam round and round him, and stroked him with their bills.

Some little children came into the garden with corn and pieces of bread, which they threw into the water; and the smallest one cried out: "There is a new one!" The other children shouted with joy, "Yes, a new one has come!" And they clapped their hands and danced about, running after their father and mother. They threw the bread into the water, and one and all said that "the new one was the prettiest; he was so young and handsome." And the old swans bent their heads and did homage before him.

He felt quite shy, and hid his head under his wing; he did not know what to think; he was so very happy, but not at all proud; a good heart never becomes proud. He thought of how he had been pursued and scorned, and now he heard them all say that he was the most beautiful of all beautiful birds. The lilacs bent their boughs right down into the water before him, and the bright sun was warm and cheering, and he rustled his feathers and raised his slender neck aloft, saying with exultation in his heart: "I never dreamt of so much happiness when I was the Ugly Duckling!"

In this
style
1016